I0555601

Suvi

Forgotten Worlds, Volume 1

Prudence MacLeod

Published by Prudence MacLeod, 2023.

S.U.V.I

by

Prudence MacLeod

(second edition)

This is a work of fiction. Similarities to real people, places, or events are entirely coincidental.

SUVI

First edition. October 28, 2023.

ISBN: 978-1927478219

Written by Prudence MacLeod.

Forgotten World

On a far-off alien world, a near naked woman sat on a cold cell floor, her eyes closed, her posture serene, patiently waiting for that cell door to open for the last time. How did she get there? It began this way.

In the year of 2221, old Earth reckoning, the first of the five great ships set out. Each ship carried ten thousand settlers, all highly skilled, extremely intelligent, people who were anxious to extend mankind's reach into the galaxy.

They all believed they would be in constant contact with the rest of the colonies, but that's not what happened. Soon after the third ship was launched, a war devastated Earth. The last two ships barely made it into open space. There were few survivors left on the home planet, and they didn't last long.

The man whose vision the great ships were, had foreseen this, and hatched a plot in secret. Each colony was dropped off then abandoned forever with no way off the world on which they had landed. Mankind had been seeded into the galaxy, and the visionary's hope was, even if only a few of the colonies managed to survive, mankind would continue to exist.

He had no way to know if he had succeeded or not, but he had. The great ships, once they'd dropped off the colonists, returned to Earth for another group of settlers, but they found it devastated and uninhabitable.

They gathered at a single ship, chose one by lots, then robbed the other four for fuel and supplies. The idea was to find a new planet to start a colony of their own from the combined crews. Mankind had perished on the home world, but lived on, alone in forgotten places.

That is, until the one ship returned. The one ship had wandered for many years until the captain gave up the search and returned to where he'd dropped off his original colonists, hoping they would welcome more settlers. It didn't go as he'd planed.

1

Chapter #1
SUVI

Farouk Bladon sighed and stared at the display screen. "So, the great ship returns."

"Yes, First Prime," said Jonah Thornton, the small man beside him. "It draws closer as we speak. There's no doubt it's returning at last. Sir, what should we do?"

Farouk seemed lost in thought. "Hmm? Do? I think we should welcome them, don't you?"

"But, Sir, what if they've brought more colonists?"

"Then we welcome them as well, they can decide for themselves what to do once we've gone. Bring SUVI 5 to me. We'll hold a feast; she can provide the meat. Tell her to wear her hunting gear."

"At once, First Prime." The man hurried away.

Farouk returned his gaze to the screen. Yes, there was no doubt, the ship would reach a docking orbit within hours. He wondered what those people on the ship would think when they found the original colony deserted. It should prove interesting."

Smiling, he turned to the other man in the room, a man wearing only a loincloth and carrying a bladed weapon. "Nineteen, my friend, destiny has smiled upon us this day. Once SUVI 5 is on her way, prepare your troops, they will be needed soon." He returned his gaze to the screen, a cold smile playing at his lips.

* * * * *

The lock clicked open, and the cell door swung wide. The near naked woman sitting cross-legged on the bare floor didn't even look up. Her eyes were closed, and she was taking deep slow breaths. Jonah Thornton shuddered then squared his shoulders and spoke. "SUVI 5, by the command of the First Prime you will don hunting gear and return to the scanner room with me. He wishes to speak to you."

She opened those glowing amber eyes. He swallowed the lump of fear in his throat as he watched those eyes slowly return to their natural green. "If I'm to hunt I'll need weapons, Second Prime."

"You'll collect your weapons before you transport to the surface, as always. You know full well you can't carry weapons in the presence of the First Prime."

"As you command," she replied as she rose and dropped her loincloth to the floor. She reached for the folded leathers on the shelf beside her and pulled on the breeks, chaps, and jerkin that she wore when hunting. She pushed her feet into thick moccasins then followed him out of the cell.

Jonah led her back to the observation room, nervously fingering the controller in his hand. He was terrified of this woman and, even though he knew full well the pain collar fastened around her neck would make her compliant, allow him to control her, he was still soaked in sweat. "First Prime, SUVI 5."

Farouk turned to give her an oily smile. "Come closer, SUVI 5. See that blip on this screen? That's the great ship, it's finally returned. I wish to have a celebration, a feast for the ship's officers. You will go to the surface and acquire meat for the feast. No small rodents now, kill something big enough to feed a few dozen people. Go now, and hunt well."

She turned and started away, but his voice called her back. "SUVI 5, do not fail me."

"As you command," she replied, showing no emotion at all, and strode away.

The woman stepped into the corridor and from there into another room where she approached a glowing platform. SUVI 19 was waiting there with her weapons, two large daggers, nothing more. She was not trusted with more, yet she was still their most successful hunter. A look of understanding passed between them as she accepted the knives from his hand, then she stepped onto the platform. There was a flash of light and she was suddenly standing on a similar platform on the planet's surface.

Drawing a deep breath of fresh air for the first time in days, SUVI 5 stepped off the platform and smiled. For the moment she was free. They wouldn't call her back until she'd completed the hunt, and she was in no hurry. Knowing they couldn't see her, she grinned with delight as she pulled the two long sharp spears from their hiding place. Excited by the destiny she sensed nearing, and ready for a run in the open air, SUVI 5 set out for the hunt.

* * * * *

"We've achieved standard orbit, Captain Baris."

"Thank you, Helmsman. Maintain Orbit. Commander Volkov, how do things look down there?"

"Dead," was the curt reply.

"What???"

"Sir, there's nothing moving down there. Place looks like it's been deserted for a long time. The habitats are completely grown over, most have been broken open. There's not a single sign of human ... wait, I've got something. There's a woman, looks like a primitive human. Sir, that looks a lot like a T-Rex chasing her."

"What??? Good Christ, get her up here, now. I'll be in the transportation bay." The order was relayed as the captain hurried from the bridge and down the corridor to the transport room. He burst through the door. "Where is she?"

"She's moving too fast, Captain; I can't get a lock on her. Shit, that things's caught up to her."

The ten people in the room held their breath as they watched the screen. The monstrous beast reached for the fleeing woman. Just as the jaws were about to close on her she dropped to the ground and braced the butt of her spear. The animal impaled itself on that shaft and the woman scrambled away as it snapped in two.

The beast was bleeding profusely, but far from dead. "Got her!" exulted the man at the controls as he threw the switch to transport her to the ship. Unfortunately, at that moment the animal charged.

The woman arrived in the transport room, but so did the beast. It attacked instantly, biting one security man in half while ripping the arm off the other. It whipped around, its tail knocking down three more people, but the woman was on its back now, her knives slashing at its throat. The animal leaped and bucked, trying to dislodge the creature that clung to it, but to no avail.

Blood sprayed everywhere, people screamed and scrambled away as best they could, and the woman kept slashing with her knives. Slowly the beast began to tire, the blood loss was taking its toll. It stopped moving and just stood still but the woman didn't stop slashing until the animal collapsed to the floor. The warrior wiped her blades on the dead animal then sheathed those deadly knives.

"Should be out of reach now," she said as she grasped the strange collar at her neck, "if not I'll lay dead beside this garog, for I'll be a slave no longer."

With a primal scream her muscles lurched, the veins on her forehead and neck stood out, throbbing. She grunted with effort as those mighty muscles writhed and bunched, and then the metal parted with a sizzle and snap of electrical connections being torn and metal breaking.

With a wild shout of joy, she threw aside the broken collar and whipped out her daggers. She took a stride towards the captain who swallowed hard, his eyes wide with fear, but she dropped the knives to the floor and knelt before him.

"Captain Baris, it's good to see you again. I'm afraid I've lost my ball, so we'll have to wait for another time to resume our game."

Chapter #2
Reunion

The captain shook off the shock and reached for the gore bespattered woman who knelt before him. "Jeannie? My god, are you little Jeannie Sorenson?"

"I was that child, before I was infected," she replied as he took her arm and raised her to her feet. "Now my designation is SUVI 5."

"Designation? What does it mean? What do you mean, you were infected?"

"Elysium holds many dangers, Captain. The ship was gone merely days when the oraks migrated through our landing site. They killed hundreds, but it was the parasite they carried that was deadlier. By the time they'd moved on over half out numbers were dead."

"Oh my god. Your mother?"

"She fell trying to protect me, but I was infected anyway. Only a handful of us survived that infection. The virus rewrites some of the DNA and rewires the brain somewhat. We are no longer considered human, we are now SUVI, survivor of unidentified viral infection. I was the fifth survivor."

"You said you were a slave," said another voice.

SUVI 5 turned to respond and grinned broadly at the young woman facing her so earnestly. "Oh my, you are so incredibly beautiful, are you the goddess of the ship?"

The girl blushed furiously and stepped back. "I'm Ensign Amanda Drake, the transportation officer."

"To answer your question, beautiful Amanda, all SUVI are indentured slaves. We're told that it cost the colony so many resources to save our lives that we must spend the duration of those lives working to repay the debt."

She turned back to the captain. "I beg you for sanctuary, Captain Baris. If you cannot grant me that, then kill me now, for I'll never go back to that stinking cavern under the ground."

"Of course I'll grant you sanctuary, Jeannie. There's much you can tell us about the colony, but first you need a chance to clean up, some new clothing, and a good meal. Ensign, take Miss Sorenson and see to her needs, find her quarters, clothing, and whatever else she needs."

"Sir."

"Captain, they'll be looking for me soon. They will also want to come up here, or for you to go down to meet with them. Please, don't do it, stall until after we've talked. Captain Baris, you're the only human to have shown me true kindness in living memory. I beg you, sir, trust no one."

With that she turned to the young ensign. "Take me away, woman of beauty, do what you will with me."

Wide eyed, Amanda looked at her. "You're flirting with me? Now? There are three dead people and a ... god only knows what that thing is, plus you're covered in blood and gore, and you're flirting with me?"

"I brought meat," grinned SUVI 5, "will you not cook it for me?"

"I most certainly will not," she huffed as she strode away. "Come on, you need a bath. We'll see about the rest once you don't smell so bad." SUVI 5 winked at the captain and followed the girl's retreating back.

SUVI 5 followed the ensign through several corridors. They drew a lot of attention, but no one spoke or interfered. Suddenly Ensign Blake stopped and turned on SUVI 5. "Are you hanging back to watch my ass?"

"You are so bewitchingly beautiful, Ensign Amanda Drake; how can I not want to gaze upon your magnificence?" came the mischievous reply.

"Woman, you and I need to talk. In here, these are your quarters. Now, the shower is through there. Clean yourself up then I'll take you to the mess for food. Ah, ah, not another word. Go."

Still grinning, SUVI 5 shed her leathers then followed the direction of the pointing arm. A moment later she screamed.

Ensign Drake ran into the small bathroom. "Are you hurt?"

"Hurt? That water is boiling; is this how I'm to be punished for teasing you?"

Amanda gazed into those fearful eyes in confusion. She reached through the steam to shut off the water before responding. "You're not being punished, SUVI 5, you just turned on the hot water without the cold."

"Hot water?"

"Hot water, don't you know how to adjust the water temperature?"

"The water for cleansing is always cold. I don't understand."

"You really don't, do you? Here, let me show you. You pull this to start the water, this you did. Now, turn it to adjust the temperature. Hard right is all cold, hard left is all hot, and what you like best is somewhere in the middle. Here, try this."

Cautiously, SUVI 5 stuck her hand into the water then smiled with delight, it was wonderfully warm, but not hot. She started to thank Amanda, but she'd already left the room. SUVI 5 sighed with delight and luxuriated under the warm water for a long time. She figured out the soaps and the rest by experimenting and old memories.

At length she turned off the water then stepped from the shower to find several soft towels. She rubbed her hair as dry as possible with one then her body with another. Exiting the bathroom wrapped in the towel she found a pile of fresh clothing on the bed and Amanda in the chair reading.

SUVI 5 dropped the towel and proceeded to dress herself in the jumpsuit and soft shoes. She sighed with delight at the new clothing. "Don't you want to dry your hair?"

"Dry my hair?"

"Let me," said Amanda as she fetched the hairdryer and a comb from the bathroom. "Sit here."

SUVI 5 sat and endured the hair drying, only making a few soft yelps as the comb caught in a stubborn tangle or two. Finally it was finished, and Amanda turned her to gaze in the mirror. "There now, isn't that better?"

"Yes," she sighed as she gazed at her freshly scrubbed face. "I have so many new things to learn." She turned to Ensign Drake, her expression no longer teasing, but somewhat self-effacing. "Forgive me, Ensign Amanda Drake. Thank you for your kindness to me, and thank you for the wonderful gift."

"Gift?"

"You allowed me to be playful with you, you treated me as an equal, and you teased me back. These things are so rare in the life of the SUVI, only possible when alone with other SUVI. To be treated so, allowed this by a full human, is a precious gift."

"SUVI 5, of course I treat you as an equal. You're as human as I am."

"No, actually, I'm not. I was once, but no longer."

Amanda Drake gazed at her for a long moment. "Hungry?"

"Yes."

"Come on then. We'll go to the mess hall and get some food into you. We can pick up that discussion while we eat. Also, how about you just call me Amanda when we're alone, or Ensign Drake when I'm on duty."

"Yes, I can do that, Amanda, if you wish it so."

"I do, now your name's Jeannie, right?"

"It was before I was infected. That life is over, that person is no more. Now I have no name, just my designation."

They had now reached the mess, but it was early, and they had the place pretty much to themselves. Amanda showed her how to access the food, made a few suggestions, then led the way to a table. "Okay, back to the name thing. You said Jeannie is no more, that life is gone."

"Yes."

"Well, so is your life as SIVU 5. You threw off the slave collar and chose sanctuary on the ship. Your life is all new again, so you need a new name. How about Suvi-jean?"

The woman's eyes lit up with delight and she gazed at Ensign with adoration. "I like that, a lot, a real name, one made up of the two people I once was. Can I do that? Can I claim that name for myself?"

"Indeed you can, my friend, indeed you can," smiled Amanda. "Now ..." She got no further as her com unit pinged. "Ensign Amanda Drake here."

"Amanda, this is the captain. How is our new passenger doing?"

"She's been assigned quarters, sir, gotten cleaned up, and now we're in the mess destroying the desserts."

"Excellent," chuckled the captain. "As soon as you're finished, bring her to the bridge, my briefing room. We'll be waiting."

"On our way, sir." She stood and gathered the empty plates. "Let's go, Suvi-jean, can't keep the captain waiting." She showed her where to put the plates then led the way to the bridge and into the captain's meeting room.

They entered to find the captain and the rest of the senior staff sitting around a huge table. Ensign Drake introduced her as Suvi-jean, then showed her to a chair. She sat with straight back and her hands folded in her lap. She made eye contact with no one.

"Well, Jeannie, has Ensign Drake got you all settled in?"

"Ensign Drake has been most kind, Captain. Yes, she has assigned a new cell where only I control the locks, there is plenty of room, and amenities I'm unfamiliar with, but anxious to explore."

"Only you control the locks?" asked a woman to the captain's right. "Sorry, I'm Olga Volkov, first officer of this ship. What do you mean, only you control the locks?"

"On the planet below, I am SUVI, not human, not trusted, not free. The cell is always locked from the outside until I am taken out for service to the community."

The room was silent for a few moments, then the captain spoke again. "That won't happen here, I promise you. Jeannie, you said you have information I should have before responding to the hails from the planet. Can you tell me what you mean?"

Suvi-jean finally lifted her chin and made eye contact with him. They could easily see the adoration in her eyes as he smiled kindly at her. "Sir, perhaps I should speak of our history. When first the settlers were landed all went well. A few days later the first wave of the Oraks appeared. They're a small creature, half the size of a grown man, herbivorous for the most part, and yet aggressive, deadly in numbers. The colony was right in the path of the migration.

"The bite of the Orak isn't poisonous as such, yet many of them carry a virus deadly to humans. Between the beasts and the virus, the colony was devastated. Less than a hundred of the infected survived that infection, and barely ten of us with a whole mind, the rest were completely mad and had to be put down.

"The colony was moved, but a year later another migration of Oraks swept through with similar results. Our leaders were all dead by that time, well, most of them. The man who originally was in charge of the small security force, managed to survive. He declared himself First Prime and used his troops to enforce his rule. The colony became a dictatorship, and the SUVI were enslaved.

"SUVI 9 found the caverns below in time to save us from a third migration. The colony was moved underground, caverns expanded, and the entrances fortified. None can enter without permission, nor can anyone leave without wearing a pain collar. Only the SUVI can survive long on the surface, and thus it is we who do the work above. We maintain the air vents and filters, we grow much of the food, and we hunt for the meat, usually me."

"Why you in particular?" asked another woman. "I'm Second Officer Naleen Raveer."

"Because I'm more successful, Second Officer Raveer."

"Why were you not carrying more effective modern weapons? I'm Chief Security Officer Brandon Hoffman."

"The SUVI are considered too dangerous to be allowed modern weapons, sir. The First Prime fears the SUVI, even though he is one."

The captain leaned forward at that. "Are you saying Farouk Bladon is a SUVI like you?"

"No sir, not like me, but he is SUVI. Captain, each SUVI is different. When infected, the virus attempts to rewrite the DNA, to mutate the host into something more adaptable, more likely to survive on the planet. However, each infected human evolves differently. Some are badly distorted, others greatly enhanced. I'm one of the latter, so is the First Prime.

"Our enhancements are quite different though. The First Prime has a devious mind. He constantly keeps the humans squabbling among themselves, battling for finite resources which he alone controls. He is unbelievably strong, has uncanny peripheral vision, and keen instincts for danger. I've tried and failed twice to kill him. So have many others. Each one was publicly executed, all except me."

"Why not you?" asked the first officer.

"He uses me for his pleasure, and he needs me to hunt. He needs a diet rich in protein, and I'm the most successful hunter."

The captain took a moment to absorb that information. "What else can you tell us?" he asked, his voice going hard.

"First Prime Bladon wants to capture this ship, or any ship for that matter. He's had me working on a ship for years. He has no idea at all I could have finished it easily at any time, but I dared not give it to him.

"He was the chief of Security before the fall, and as First Prime he retains that small force to ensure the obedience of the citizens. Only the Security men are allowed modern weapons."

"Do you know why he wants a ship so badly?"

"He wants to return to Earth. Captain, we dare not let him return there, he's far too dangerous."

"Jeannie, there is no Earth anymore. It's scorched, nothing can live there now."

"That is sad news indeed," she replied, her shoulders sagging. "I too had hoped to go there where I might be allowed to live free. He won't believe you, though. He's obsessed with the idea. In truth I think it's his virus wanting all those billions of possible hosts."

"What about your virus?" asked another man. "I'm chief medical officer, Dr. Eamon Reilly.

"My virus is inert, Dr."

"You're certain of that?"

"I am, yes."

"How can you tell for certain?"

"I was sent to the surface to hunt. I arrived just after a migration of Oraks had gone through. I saw many sick animals, but they all searched out a certain berry bush and ate the berries. I watched and the next day they appeared to be fine. Having nothing to lose, I ate some of the berries, got sick for a few hours, then my mind cleared for the first time since I'd been infected.

"Each time I go hunting now, I sneak a few berries back to the other SUVI. Slowly but surely the rest have become clear again, all except Farouk Bladon. He has no idea how this is happening, and frets while he waits for it to happen for him."

"Can you tell us anything more about your differences, your unique abilities?" asked Dr. Reilly.

When she didn't answer, just looked away, the captain leaned his elbows on the table and spoke kindly. "Please, Jeannie. We'll honor the sanctuary, but on the ship, everybody must take up certain tasks, help maintain the ship. Also, the doctor should know all there is about you in case someday you need his help. We're not going to lock you up or blow you out the air lock in fear. Please trust me, I promise you'll be safe and respected here."

She sighed and squared her shoulders. "All right, Captain. I'll trust you, and ask for your trust in return. I swear I will never bring danger to you, this ship, or its personnel. My unique abilities are this: I'm stronger than any human, faster, and more agile. I can sense danger approaching, I'm highly intuitive, I have exceptional vision and hearing, I learn new things incredibly fast, and I forget nothing.

"I have a strong sense of forewarning. For example, I knew the ship was nearing days before anyone else. I knew I'd be sent out hunting, so I used yet another talent. I have full genetic memory."

"Full genetic memory," said Dr. Reilly, sitting forward in his chair. "Explain."

"I need to focus, but I can recall experiences and abilities of any of my ancestors. For the hunt I focus on the skills of a hunter/gatherer. As I fled from the garog, I had a strong sense of needing to save humans from it, so I focused on a warrior ancestor. It was that divided attention that nearly allowed it to get me. It was the warrior that killed it. The hunter would have used the second spear. Ensign Drake, forgive me, it was the warrior who flirted so shamelessly with you." Amanda blushed, but didn't speak.

"Wow, so, is that everything?" asked the Second Officer.

"There could be more, but I've never been allowed to explore the possibilities."

"Can we get back to the small ship for a moment?" asked the Chief Engineer. "You said you could easily finish it. Trying to create a small ship that will function in an atmosphere as well as space plus give it super light engines all by yourself is a near impossible task. When did you get your engineering education?"

"I didn't," replied Suvi-jean. "I focused on my mother's skill set before starting work each time."

"Ah yes," smiled the captain. "Helena Sorenson was a hell of an engineer. Well people, what do you think?"

"Assign her to Engineering, Captain," grinned Chief Engineer Moira Duncan. "I've got a project or two I'd like her to take a look at."

"I'll have her in Security with that physical skill set of hers," grinned the Security Chief.

"Relax, Jeannie, relax," said the captain as he saw her tense up. "You're not a slave here, and these greedy characters aren't trying to claim you as property, they want your help. Jeannie, we've taken you in, now we're just trying to find a place where you can fit. Find your place, as it were. Have you any idea what you might like to do?"

"Do? I don't understand."

Ensign Drake spoke up then. "Suvi-jean, for eight hours each day, I'm the transport officer. I have a desk where I do much of my work, but I may have other errands to do elsewhere. Of the remaining sixteen hours I try to sleep seven and have nine hours for myself, meals, hanging out with friends, other activities."

A naughty grin began to play at Suvi-jean's lips. "Oh yes, those other activities ..."

Amanda Drake shook a warning finger at her. "Oh no, don't you even think about starting that again, especially not here." Finally she laughed.

"Suvi-jean, that's what these people are trying to help you decide. Each one of these people is head of their own department. They want to know if you have the skills, or the desire, to work in their department. Eight hours of work then sixteen for yourself, just like everybody else, same and equal."

Suvi-jean visibly relaxed, nodding her head as understanding reached her awareness. "I'm sorry for the paranoia, Captain. I promise I'll do my best wherever I'm assigned."

The Captain seemed to be lost in thought and no one disturbed him. Finally he spoke as his attention returned to the room. "Suvi-jean,

I hereby assign you the rank of Ensign. You will report directly to me. Your task is as follows, spend time in each department of the ship, use your intuitive senses to get a feel for things, then, if you see places we might improve, or have ideas we might try, bring them to me first.

"Ensign Drake, assist Ensign Sorenson to settle in, get her a proper uniform, show her the ropes, get her started, that sort of thing. Jeannie, I can usually be found on the bridge if you need me."

"Not in the corridors playing dance with the ball?" she grinned in reply.

He laughed heartily at that. "No, not since our last encounter, Jeannie. Now, off you go, settle in. Take your time, Jeannie, there's no rush."

"Thank you, Captain. People, thank you all for your acceptance, and your patience with me. I'm sure I'll test that patience many times as I find my way. I swear I will always ask permission before entering any department, nor will I ever attempt to override or subvert the authority you hold. I want to learn how I can be of service to the ship, no more than that."

With that they all filed out. As they did, Moira Duncan stepped up beside her. "I was serious about those projects I want you to look at."

Suvi-jean took a quick look at Moira's name tag. "Yes, Commander Duncan. I admit I was intrigued by that. Your department will be one of my first stops."

"Take time to settle in, girl," replied Moira, "then look me up." She was whistling a merry tune as she marched briskly away.

As Amanda led Suvi-Jean away, the captain called the First Officer and the Chief of Security back. "Captain?"

"Olga, I remember Farouk Bladon from the original voyage. He wasn't a particularly likeable man. There should be information in the archives to help us. Both of you see what you can find."

"So, you believe her story, Captain?"

"Don't you?"

"Well, she did kill that monster with a knife, but it took out two of my men armed with modern weapons," sighed Brandon Hoffman. "So the part about her physical attributes stands up. I've sent the remains of that collar to Engineering for analysis. Let's see what they've learned."

He reached for his comm unit. "Security to Engineering."

"Moira here. What's up, Brandon?"

"Have you had a look at that broken collar of Jeannie Sorenson's yet?"

"Sure have. The little bugger is ringed with electrical contact points. I sure as hell wouldn't want to be wearing it when it's activated."

"Thanks, Moira, Brandon out. Well, Captain, that part seems to stand up too. I'm willing to say she's told us the truth."

"So am I," agreed the captain.

"Captain?"

"You heard her, Brandon. That collar was used to make her compliant, she said Farouk used her for his pleasure. That I can believe about him. I trust the girl. We'll stall for a while and see how this plays out."

Chapter #3

Ensign Suvi-jean

"I'll show you back to your quarters," said Amanda.

"I can find it," replied Suvi-jean.

"You can?"

"I don't forget anything, remember? You brought me here from the eating place, so I retrace my steps there and then to the room. Yes?"

"Yes, that'll work, but I'll show you a faster way." She set out with Suvi-jean right beside her. "Perhaps you should spend the first few days just learning your way around the ship."

"Memorizing the pathways, familiarizing myself with the new environment, yes, I like this plan. Will you be showing me around, or will I explore on my own?"

Amanda smiled. "Which would you prefer?" Noticing the sudden grin on the woman's face she shook a finger at her. "Just you forget that. God, you're full of mischief." She suddenly went serious. "Suvi-jean, is this your true nature finally asserting itself?"

To Amanda's surprise, Suvi-jean answered seriously. "I don't really know, Amanda. I don't. Perhaps it is, I hope it might be."

"Really?"

"Yes, really," grinned Suvi-jean. "Amanda, the face I showed the world was always a face of controlled power, projecting an aura of danger. Only with the other SUVI could I dare to be like this, let my guard down, but those opportunities were rare. In truth, I have no idea what my true self is like. She's as much a mystery to me as she is to you."

They'd stopped walking and now Amanda turned to continue down a different corridor. "Suvi-jean, can you tell me why you chose me to be playful with?"

"I instinctively felt you wouldn't hurt me, or be offended by my playfulness. The instant I saw you I knew and couldn't stop myself. That part of me so aches for a chance to exist."

"Ah-huh. You're sure that's it?"

"Yes it ..., hey you, I'm the bad SUVI, remember, I do the teasing." She spotted the small grin playing at Amanda's lips.

Amanda burst out laughing. "Okay, but it's a lot more fun teasing you. Ah, here we are back at your quarters. Come on in and I'll show you how some of the things work. Do you recognize any of the amenities?"

"Yes, most of them. I was born on this ship, and I can access my mother's memories of the things I need here."

Amanda grinned. "Okay, show me."

Suvi-jean closed her eyes and took a deep breath. Her eyes opened, glowing amber, and she sat to the computer. "Awaken."

The screen lit up and a voice spoke. "Name, rank, and request please."

"Suvi-jean, rank of Ensign. These are my quarters; this terminal is for my use only."

"Noted and confirmed. Welcome, Ensign Suvi-jean Sorenson. What is your request?"

"Show me the schematics for the entire ship." The original blueprints popped up on the screen. "Floor plan only." The display adjusted. "So, I arrived at the transport room here, we went to the quarters here, then to the mess hall, then to the bridge, then returned by this route." She was tracing the pathways with her finger.

"Thank you, computer. Sleep now. So, what do you think, Amanda?"

Amanda smiled and headed for the door. "I think you'll be just fine on your own. It's nearly time for my sleep cycle. I suggest you get some rest too."

"So, now you rest, then you have nine hours for yourself?"

"No, when I awaken it will be time to work, then I'll have my off time."

"Amanda, did you spend all your personal time with me this day?"

"At the captain's request, yes. That's the nature of life as a ship's officer." A look of sad disappointment crossed Suvi-jean's face. "Suvi-jean, relax, it was no hardship for me to spend time with you."

"Ensign Amanda Drake, again I owe you thanks for your kindness. I fully understand the concept of friendship, but I have never experienced the phenomenon. Will you and I become friends, do you think?"

Amanda gave her a gentle smile. "I think we're off to a good start."

"Special friends?" asked Suvi, a naughty smile teasing at her lips.

Amanda gave a soft laugh then stepped through the door. "Good night, Suvi-jean."

"Good night, Amanda Drake, my friend," breathed Suvi-jean as the door closed. She stripped off her jumpsuit and crawled onto the soft bed. She couldn't remember ever having enjoyed the luxury of an actual bed. Feeling safe for the first time in memory, she fell into an exhausted sleep. Battling the garog had seriously depleted her reserves.

* * * * *

For three full days Suvi-jean prowled the ship, rarely stopping to eat, and taking only short sleeps. Her activities had drawn attention. Chief Security Officer Hoffman approached the captain, requesting a private audience. They retreated to the briefing room.

"All right, Brandon, what's on your mind?"

"Sir, it's Ensign Suvi-jean."

"Oh, what's she done?"

"Sir, she's spent the past three days memorizing the entire ship. According to the central computer she's spent considerable time studying the ship's schematics. Captain, I'm becoming uneasy about this. You said yourself that the talks with the grounders wasn't going well."

"You think she's spying on us for Farouk?"

"Sir, they're both SUVI. I ..."

The captain's com unit pinged. "Captain Baris."

"Sir, it's Suvi-jean. Can you spare some time for me?"

"Of course, Jeannie."

"Could Commander Hoffman join us, my observations will be of interest to his department."

"He's here with me now, Jeannie. We're in the briefing room, can you find it?"

"On my way, sir."

The captain raised his eyes to his Security Chief. "Well, here comes your answers." A moment later there was a soft tap on the door. "Enter."

Suvi-jean entered and smiled shyly. "Captain, Commander Hoffman."

"What's on your mind, Jeannie?" asked the captain.

"Captain, I have a strong sense that you will allow the First Prime to visit the ship. I advise against this. However, I foresee that it will happen, so we need to prepare." She turned to the computer. "Computer, may we have a full schematic of this ship displayed?"

The wall screen lit up with the display. "When they activate their transporters, the SUVI, as well as the security forces, will transport to different parts of the ship."

"How do you know this?" demanded Commander Hoffman.

"The First Prime has been overheard making such plans before. It's my estimation they'll arrive at several vital systems simultaneously." She reached up and tapped the display with a finger. "Here is where we're most vulnerable, and here as well."

"The air and water processors?" asked Commander Hoffman. "Why there? Why not engineering, or the armory?"

"Those will be attacked as well, but the main thrust will be to shut down the air and water processors."

"Why?"

"Humans cannot survive long without air or water. A few may survive the lack of air by the means of small back up units, but even they will soon perish without water. Once all are dead the ship can be taken over, revived, and he is free to go his way."

"That's utter madness," exclaimed the captain. "Kill the entire ship's compliment? Even Farouk Bladon wouldn't ..."

"He's done it before," she replied quietly.

"Jeannie, what do you mean, he's done it before?"

"When first we found the caverns, they were too small to accommodate all of us. The SUVI, the security forces, engineers, and medics were transported down, anyone else he needed or wanted, and the rest left to die on the surface. Within a month none remained. Captain, I beg you, prepare for the worst. If I'm wrong then no harm is done, but ..."

"Sweet Jesus," breathed Commander Hoffman. "Is that what you've been doing the past three days, looking for weaknesses?"

"Yes. I tried to seek you out at first, but was told you were too busy, so I went looking for information I thought you should have."

Hoffman squared his shoulders. "All right, what are we likely to be facing at these vulnerable points?"

"If you face the security forces, then you face humans equipped with conventional weapons. If you face the SUVI you face superior physical beings with only bladed weapons. They will be stronger, faster, and utterly ruthless. They'll strike hard and fast, then expect to be transported out before they die without air."

"Suggestions?"

"The SUVI are the more dangerous opponents, but conventional weapons can damage the exterior hull. You are more likely to understand what to do against them. Against the SUVI have your people armed with stun gas and tranquilizer darts or stunners. They'll be susceptible to these. Also, your people should have armor that will stop a blade driven by a strong hand."

"Got it," said Commander Hoffman. "Ensign Suvi-jean ..."

"You were aware of my movements and feared I was looking for ways to sabotage the ship," she said, a small grin playing at her mouth.

"Yes."

"Excellent, that tells me you're good at your job. I will report my observation to the captain immediately."

Commander Hoffman laughed at that. "Suvi-jean, are you sure you don't want to sign on with security?"

"I'll consider it," she smiled. "Captain, please tell me we have time to prepare."

"You do. We're still negotiating the terms of their visit. I did notice the First Prime insisted on visiting the ship first. What would have happened if I'd gone down?"

"You'd have been used as a lever to gain access to the ship, and then killed. Taking the ship by surprise is much faster, and thus the preferred tactic. However, I believe Commander Hoffman will have counter measures in place when needed."

The captain was visibly shaken, but he recovered quickly. "So, have you got any advice for an old captain?"

"Turn the ship away, move it out of range of his transporters as quickly as possible."

He sighed and sank into his chair. "I can't, Jeannie. If what you say is true, and I believe it is, there are people down there who would probably be thrilled to get off that planet and back to a more civilized life."

"Approximately seven hundred, yes."

"We can't just abandon them, Jeannie. We have to save them if we can."

She pressed her lips tightly together then nodded. "Then we need to prepare. Commander Hoffman, is there any way I can be of assistance to you?"

"I'm sure there is," he replied. "With your permission, Captain, we'll be about the task."

"Do it, Brandon. Do it quickly."

The commander nodded. "Come along, Ensign Suvi-jean. From now until this is over you're my special adviser." He led the way out and she followed close behind.

* * * * *

"Here comes Jake," said Carla Marks, one of the three people sitting at the table relaxing over a meal. They looked up to see a tall lanky man approaching. His upper body seemed to float high above the unnaturally long legs that appeared to move independently of the rest of the man. Each leg seemed to flip out one huge foot then the other flipped a foot. He approached the table and slid into a seat in one disjointed motion.

"Hey, Amanda," he grinned. "Where's your new girlfriend?"

Amanda raised her head to meet his gaze. "Excuse me?"

"Suvi-jean, the captain's pet."

The other man spoke up. "Careful, Jake. I was in the transport room when she arrived with that fucking dinosaur, or whatever the hell that thing was. Ensign Suvi-jean will eat you for breakfast and still be hungry."

Jake grinned at his brother, Hal. "So that's where she's been hanging out, at Security?"

"Yeah, she's got Commander Hoffman reorganizing the whole department. My ribs may never heal."

"Hal?" That was Amanda. "What do you mean, your ribs may never heal?"

"What did you do?" asked Carla. "Did you mouth off to Suvi-jean and get your ass kicked?"

"She was explaining what we'd face in a battle with the SUVI. She said they'd be wearing only loincloths and carrying knives. I snorted, I mean, we have stunners and wear armor. Seriously?"

Amanda grinned. "So, what happened?"

"I swear to god, I didn't see her move. First thing I knew I was flying through the air, landed on my back with her on my chest, one knife at my throat and the others at my balls. She hopped back and told me to defend myself. Did you know that our body armor has eleven weak points? I do, I've got a bruise on each one. The woman's not fucking human."

"No, she's not," said Amanda. "Seriously. She told me herself that her DNA has been rewritten so she's not completely human anymore. However, I'm sure the point she was trying to make was not to underestimate the SUVI in a fight, because none of them are human."

"Yeah, well, point taken," grumbled Hal.

"So, where is she?" asked Jake. "I understood the two of you were inseparable."

"Shut up, Jake," sighed Amanda. "Actually, I haven't seen her in days."

"Feeling lonely?"

"I said shut up. God."

She endured more of their teasing then everybody said goodnight and sought out their own quarters. As Amanda reached her door she found Suvi-jean sitting on the floor beside it. "Suvi-jean? What are you doing here?"

"Amanda, I've come to apologize and beg forgiveness."

Amanda gave her a quizzical look then opened the door. "Come inside and tell me all about it." Suvi-jean rose with a liquid grace and followed. She sat where Amanda indicated, then was handed a water container. "You prefer water, right?"

"Correct, and thank you."

"So, what am I forgiving you for?" asked Amanda as she sat in the chair facing Suvi-jean.

"I fear I got lost in my self-appointed tasks, and neglected my one and only friend. Forgive me if I promise not to do it again?"

The sincerity of the apology startled Amanda. She took a moment to remind herself this woman had no frame of reference. In all her life this former slave had never had a friend, not a single one. "There's nothing to forgive. Suvi-jean, we don't have to spend every moment together. If we go days with seeing each other, we'll still be friends."

"You promise? You're not upset with me?"

"Not even a little bit, girl, but I am curious as to what you've been up to. Come on now, tell me all about your adventures. I know you beat up one of the security guys. What else did you do?"

Suvi-jean chuckled at that. "I hope I didn't hurt him. I could see they didn't believe me about the SUVI. Just because they wear no armor, nor do they carry modern weapons, doesn't mean they'll be easy prey."

"He got the message."

"How do you know this, Amanda?"

"Hal's a friend of mine. We were just having a snack before sleep time and he spoke of it."

"Oh dear."

"Suvi-jean, it's okay. Hal's got a few bruises, and his ego back in place. There's no harm done at all. Now, can you tell me what's going on?" Are we expecting an attack from the SUVI?"

"Yes, well, I'm expecting that. I've managed to convince the captain and Commander Hoffman that it's best to prepare for the attack whether it comes or not."

"Makes sense to me. Is that why so many security guys are crammed into my poor transportation room?"

"Crammed in?"

"We've barely got room to breathe."

"That's a waste of resources. That room isn't a high priority target. I'll see if I can get a few of those people reassigned."

"Seriously? You can do that?"

"I believe I can. This would please you?"

"It would. Look, don't do anything to jeopardize the ship or endanger my people, but if all those guys aren't needed there ..."

"They are truly needed elsewhere. I'll see to it first thing after sleep period."

"Thanks. So, what else have you done?"

"Not so much. I memorized the layout of the ship, so I could find my way around, then focused on the security issue. Once we escape the danger presented by this planet, I plan to seek out the chief Engineer. She mentioned projects that caught my interest."

"Oh, what sort of projects?"

Suvi-jean smiled. "I have no idea, but she seemed so enthusiastic I was intrigued. Now, for another question. After sleep time, will you share a meal with me before we run off to work?"

"Are you asking me for a date?" Amanda instantly felt contrite. Obviously, this woman had no idea what she was talking about.

"Is that what you call such a sharing of time and pleasure? Excellent, it's a date. I should go to my rest as well." She rose and stepped to the door. "Until the morning." With a bright smile she was gone.

Gazing at the now closed door, Amanda sighed. "Well, that didn't quite go as planned. Shit. I'd better be careful here; this girl has no real idea how to interact with humans on a social level." She prepared then crawled into the bed, but sleep was a long time coming.

Next morning Amanda rose and swiftly prepared for the day. She usually didn't bother with a full meal before work, but Suvi-jean was expecting to see her at the mess. She dressed quickly and bolted through the door then shrieked. Suvi-jean was standing right outside the door.

With a hand over her heart, Amanda drew a few deep breaths. "Dammit, Suvi-jean, you scared the crap out of me."

"I'm so sorry, Amanda. I didn't mean to frighten you. I ..."

"Easy girl, easy, I'm fine, I'm okay. You just startled me; I wasn't expecting you here. I thought you'd already be at the mess. It's okay, honestly."

"Forgive me, Amanda. I just wanted to walk with you to have more time in your company. Did I do wrong?"

"Oh no, it's just ... oh fuck it." Amanda threw an arm around Suvi-jean's waist and gave her a friendly squeeze. "Come on, buddy of mine, let's go get something to eat."

As they walked along Suvi-jean spoke again. "Amanda, I'm a bit confused. This learning to be fully human is much harder than I thought it would be."

Amanda laughed at that. "Yeah, tell me about it. Most of us humans haven't figured it out yet either. Hey look, there's Hal, Carla, and Jake. I'll introduce you." She didn't notice the slightly disappointed look that fleetingly crossed Suvi-jean's face.

* * * * *

"You sent for me, First Prime?"

"I did, Jonah. The captain of the ship is still stalling me. I'm getting uneasy about this, recall SUVI 5. I have a new mission for her." Only silence greeted him. Farouk Bladon turned to cast a withering eye on his second in command. "Did you hear me, Jonah? I said to recall SUVI 5."

The smaller man didn't speak, nor would he meet his master's eyes. Finally he swallowed hard and replied. "I can't, sir."

"And just why can't you follow a simple instruction?" asked the First Prime, taking a step closer.

"She's dead," came the soft reply.

That stopped Farouk Bladon in his tracks. "Dead? No. No, no, no, it can't be. Tell me all of it."

"She'd barely gone topside when her tracker failed."

"Her tracker? The chip failed? How can that be?"

"My best guess, First Prime, is the stomach acid of a beast, probably a garog."

"Yes, she hunts them if possible, she knows how I enjoy the garog meat. Activate her slave collar, that should tell us where she died."

Jonah fiddled with the controller for a moment then shook his head. "No response, sir."

"No response? That thing should respond even if she's dead."

"Unless it's been separated from the body," said Jonah. "The Garog must have bitten her head completely off."

"SUVI 5 dead," said Farouk Bladon as he slumped into a chair. "I wouldn't have believed it possible. What am I going to do now?"

"Sir?"

"What? Oh, yes, ah, I was thinking about the capture plans. I was counting on SUVI 5 to lead the assault on the air processors. I guess I'll have to assign SUVI 13 to that now." He continued to mutter to himself, lost in his grief, and Jonah slipped out of the office, closing the door tightly behind him.

Even as the First Prime sat mourning the loss of his favorite slave, SUVI 13 found the dead garog. A quick look around showed him something else. Upon close inspection it proved to be a smashed tracking chip. A wolfish grin crossed his face as he realized SUVI 5 had cut the chip from her own neck and smashed it. The big question was, had she managed to remove the pain collar. He hoped she had.

SUVI 13 carefully buried the shattered chip then marked the dead garog as his own kill. It was an easy hunt, and First Prime would reward him for bringing his preferred meat. Better yet, somewhere out there, SUVI 5 was still alive, there was still hope. Grinning, he picked and ate some of the berries that cleared the mind.

Chapter #4

New Friends

They picked up their food and joined Amanda's friends at the table. The others fell silent as they arrived. "Guys, this is my friend, Suvi-jean. Suvi-jean, this is Carla, this is Jake, and Hal you've met already."

They muttered politely, but didn't make eye contact at first. Jake started to speak, but all he said was "Ow."

Suvi-jean looked puzzled. "Carla, why did you kick Jake under the table? Is that some sort of game you play?"

Startled, Carla looked her in the eye at last. "I was trying to keep him from getting hurt by mouthing off where he shouldn't. How did you know I did that?"

"It was quite stealthy," grinned Suvi-jean. "Your upper body barely moved, but there were vibrations under the table and it made a sound when you connected, so did Jake. Now, Jake, you were about to engage me in conversation, and Carla feared I might be offended and harm you, correct? Shall we declare the food table neutral ground where all may speak freely without physical repercussions?"

"Okay," agreed Jake, drawing the word out slowly.

"What did you want to say to me?"

"I'm just wondering who and what you are, Suvi." Jake was startled at how swiftly she stiffened, her eyes going dark and hard as flint. "I'm sorry, what did I ..."

He reached for her hand, but Amanda grabbed his wrist to prevent him. "Jake, her name is Suvi-jean, not Suvi. A SUVI is a slave, and Suvi-jean is that no longer."

He looked at Amanda who still held his wrist tightly, then back to Suvi-jean. Jake withdrew his arm. "Suvi-jean, I apologize, I meant no offense. I didn't know."

"Accepted," she said, slightly relaxing her posture. "Why did you try to touch me?"

"Again, I apologize. It was a reflex. I saw you tense up, knew I'd committed an offense, and reached to offer comfort, a connection, to hold your attention while I apologized. I meant you no harm. I also shortened your name when I spoke, not to insult, but as an expression of friendship. Jake is short for Jakob, Mandy is short for Amanda, Lala is short for Carla, and Hal is short for Harold."

"Accepted," she said, relaxing at last. "The captain still calls me Jeannie, as I was when I was a child. Will that be acceptable as a short version of my name?"

"Perfect," sighed Jake, leaning back in his chair. "Thank you, Jeannie."

"Jake, I sense resentment in you, as I have in many people on this ship. I believe I understand. The ship contains a limited number of ranking posts, and with a small society, as in the ships compliment, it must be extremely difficult for someone to rise through the ranks. Suddenly I appear, a stranger, granted rank, and promoted to be the captain's eyes and ears throughout the ship. Is this assessment correct?"

"Yeah, it is," he nodded.

"So, you want all my dread secrets."

She was smiling now, and he relaxed. "Absolutely, every last one."

"All right, let me see. I was the first child born on this ship, the captain and I became friends over a game of chase the ball in the days before we were delivered to the surface of the planet. When the disasters fell I was infected, and was one of only nineteen people to survive the virus.

"That virus rewrites the DNA trying to create a better host, a host more adaptable and able to survive on the planet. The survivors were enslaved once the humans figured out what we had become. SUVI means survivor of unknown viral infection. My slave designation was SUVI 5, the fifth survivor.

"I arrived back on the home ship in the company of an angry and wounded garog. I managed to keep it from killing everyone in the room then tore off the slave collar and begged the captain for sanctuary, which he granted. Once Captain Baris learned of my special abilities, he gave me rank and position."

Jake sighed and leaned his elbows on the table. "So that's it, you've always been the captain's pet."

Both Amanda and Carla sucked in their breath at that, but Suvi-jean spotted the tiny grin on his face. She matched it with one of her own. "You know it, mister, so you just behave yourself."

He chuckled at that and leaned closer to her. "Are you going to tell me about some of those special abilities?"

Suvi-jean leaned closer to him until they were close enough to kiss. "Not today," she whispered loudly then leaned back in her chair. This time he laughed aloud and relaxed back in his seat as well. The ice was broken, and Amanda sighed with relief. That had been pretty tense for a moment, and she regretted introducing them without talking to each in turn first.

"Great," muttered Hal, "you she flirts with, me she tried to kill."

Suvi-jean spun to face him, but saw he was smiling. "I'm so very sorry to have hurt you, Hal," she grinned. "Is there anything I can do to help you heal from such trauma?"

"Well, you could kiss make better."

She froze for a moment then a memory from her childhood kicked in and she smiled wickedly. "Are you suggesting I kiss your bruises to help them heal, or are you suggesting I kiss you to take your mind off the pain."

"Both would be real nice," he grinned in reply.

"I think you're doing quite well on your own," she chuckled. "Carla, I sense great fear of me. What can I do to reassure you that you are safe?"

"I'm sorry. Can you tell us more about the infection, the virus?"

"Of course. This is what I know. It's a parasite, as all viruses are, it rewrote a portion of my DNA making my body become more adaptable to Elysium's environment, then it went dormant. It was transmitted to me through an open wound, it changed me, then has been rendered dormant by my body. I'm not contagious, Carla. You're safe with me."

"I'm sorry, Suvi-jean, I am."

"No, you were right to be cautious, all of you. I'm alien, different, new to your environment, and you are quite right to be cautious. I hope that in time, as we become friends, spend time getting to know about each other, that you'll relax with me, learn to trust that you're safe with me."

"Is that why the SUVI were enslaved? People were afraid of you?" asked Jake.

"Yes, on several levels, and with good reason. First, they were afraid of being infected themselves, for most people died of the infection. Second, most of the survivors went insane, became violent, and had to be killed, but they caused a lot of damage and killed many before it was over. The SUVI were enslaved to repay the colony for damage done and resources lost."

"Oh my god," breathed Carla, "and you managed to survive all that."

"I did, yes."

"Suvi-jean, do you really believe the colony will send the SUVI to attack us?"

"Yes. I expect the SUVI to come as well as the security forces. They will try to capture the ship."

"What do you think would happen if they succeed?" asked Amanda.

"If they succeed the First Prime will keep the people he needs to operate the ship, and his forces to control them. The rest would be transported to the surface to fend for themselves."

"Oh my god," Carla gasped again. "Suvi, I mean Jeannie, can you stop them?"

"Yes, we can, and we will. This ship is my home, I was born here, and this is the only place I've ever felt safe. I won't allow anything to happen to this ship, or her people. They will come, we'll defeat them, and then we'll leave this planet of misery."

"We should just leave now," grumbled Jake.

"I did suggest that to the captain, but he refused. There are about seven hundred civilians alive in the caverns, and the captain wants to bring them up to the ship, to save them. He won't change his mind, so we must prepare."

"I guess I should go start preparing then," said Carla. "I work in the infirmary."

Suvi-jean, nodded and smiled reassuringly at her, then turned back to Jake. "Where do you work, Jake?"

"I take care of the crap and garbage."

"Jake," Amanda admonished gently.

"It's true, Mandy. No sense trying to deny it."

"So, you work in Sanitation?" asked Suvi-jean.

"Yup, that I do."

"That is a most important department. Without an efficient sanitation department, the ship would soon fail to function properly, or disease could run rampant," said Suvi-jean. "I will one day soon visit that department. When I do, you can show me around, Jake."

"It'll be my pleasure, pretty lady," he said, a lascivious grin playing at his lips.

"Be careful what you wish for, tall man," laughed Suvi-jean as she stood to go. "Amanda, shall we walk to Transportation together, I must start my day there."

"I'll join you," said Hal as he rose stiffly to his feet. "I'm stationed there as well."

A flicker of annoyance crossed Suvi-jean's face, but quickly vanished. The others didn't catch it, but Amanda did. As they walked along, Suvi-jean reached for her comm unit. "Ensign Sorenson to Commander Hoffman."

"Hoffman here."

"Sir, I see we have several men stationed in the transportation room. I don't believe that to be a high priority target for the grounders. Sir, I'd like to move a few of them to the water filtration plant."

"Put 'em where you want 'em, Suvi-jean. I'll authorize it."

"Thank you, Sir. Sorenson out. Hal, you're the squad leader for the men in Transport, right?"

"Yes."

"Leave two there and take the rest to the water filtration plant. You have personal experience against a SUVI in combat, so I want you in charge of the men at that station."

"Yes ma'am," he said as they reached to door to the transportation room. He stepped through the door and began issuing orders. Suvi-jean gave Amanda a shy smile then walked away.

* * * * *

Amanda looked for Suvi-jean after she got off shift, but she couldn't find her. She gave it up and hung out at the mess, but her three buddies joined her there and that's wasn't quite what she had in mind. She excused herself and left.

Suvi-jean arrived back at her quarters to find Amanda sitting by the door, reading from a tablet. "Amanda, that floor can't be comfortable, believe me, I know. Please come inside." She opened the door and led the way. Indicating that Amanda should sit, she passed her a container of Amanda's favorite sweet drink.

"Hey, this is my favorite. You like this too?"

"No, I stocked it for you when you visit me," smiled Suvi-jean. "I asked at the mess about what you'd like." She turned to the computer terminal. "Computer, awaken."

"Greetings, Ensign Sorenson, what is your request?"

"Grant full access to these quarters to Ensign Amanda Drake from this moment forward."

"Noted and established."

"Thank you, computer. Rest now. There now, Amanda, you can wait for me in comfort whenever you wish from now on."

"Thank you, Jeannie. You didn't have to do that."

"You're my friend. I want you to be comfortable, to feel welcome here in my private space." She chose a container of water for herself then sat facing Amanda. "So, there's something on your mind and it concerns me. Did I do something wrong this morning when I met your friends?"

"No, Jeannie, no. I'll admit it was a bit tense there for a while, but you were so open with them, so forthcoming in trying to allay their fears, especially with Jake. Jake's a hard case, bitter, and doesn't have a lot of friends."

"Oh? Do people find his natural forward nature unattractive?"

"Yeah, a lot do. He doesn't mean any harm, but he sure can be intrusive and annoying." Suvi-jean just nodded. "Jeannie, I got the impression something was wrong this morning."

"Oh no, ..."

"Bull. I screwed up, didn't I? You were laughing and having fun until we reached the mess then you went cold, reserved, professional, but definitely reserved. Also, you avoided making eye contact with me."

"All right, I admit it, I was hoping we would have personal time together, just us two, just for a short time and a meal. I confess I was disappointed, plus I could feel the fear and resentment from them like knives in my back. I apologize if I was too defensive."

"No, you weren't, honey. You're right, you asked me for some private time, and I blew that."

"It's okay, Amanda. I did some fast research and I realize it was perfectly acceptable to bring chaperons on the first date."

"What??? Why you, miserable beast, you ..." She threw a cushion at Suvi-jean who laughed and caught the missile. "Suvi-jean, I'm really sorry. You wanted to talk about something, and I screwed it up."

"No problem."

"Yes, it is a problem," sighed Amanda. "I know you didn't grow up on the ship, and have no real experience with social situations. I threw you in deep right off the bat, then sat feeling like a fool, leaving you to struggle with it on your own. I'm afraid I'm being a bad friend."

"Lucky for you you're so devastatingly beautiful, I'd forgive you anything just for a few minutes of your company, a glimpse of that dazzling smile."

Amanda just stared at her wide eyed and open mouthed for a moment. She swallowed hard then shook her head, and blushing furiously, laughed. "My god, Suvi-jean, where do you get that flattery from?"

"An ancestor," she grinned in reply.

"An ancestor?"

"Full genetic memory, remember? There was a male ancestor, from a history period called the Victorian Era, who was a master of the art. I was nearly struck dumb when I first saw you, Amanda. I'd never seen a human so perfect. I've been exploring the art of flattery so I can complement you properly."

Once again Amanda was blushing. "There's not a shred of guile in you, is there?" she breathed.

"Oh, I can use guile, have no fear, but never with you. Can I call you Mandy like your friends do?"

"What? Of course you can, you're my friend too."

"Then my day is a success."

"Jeannie, what was it you originally wanted to talk to me about?"

"It wasn't all that important, I just wanted to spend some time with you, just us two. I was going to ask you to help me learn more about how to act in social situations, but I got a firsthand lesson right off the mark. Serves me right, I guess."

"Serves you right? Why?"

"Well, I gave Hal a lesson right up front. I should be willing to face the same treatment, shouldn't I?"

"I suppose. Honey, just what's going through your mind. You said you wanted time with me, just us two. Tell me what's going on here for you?"

"Please don't be afraid of me, Mandy. I can feel you tensing up, pulling back from me. Please don't ever do that."

"Jeannie, I ..."

"Hush now, let me answer your question. Mandy, from the first moment I saw you I felt we belonged to each other in some special way, like close siblings, parent and child, close friends, something. It was strong, telling me this woman is a part of you, what you will become, she is precious, cherish her. The more I see you the stronger that feeling gets. I want to spend time with you, to savor the sweetness of that feeling, to understand it. Do you know what this is?"

"Suvi-jean, I like you, I do. I enjoy your company too. Honey, I know you're exploring the new you right now, all the new experiences, the new feelings, I just don't want you to get hurt, not in any way."

"But?"

"Not a but, an and. And I'm so terribly afraid I might be the one to bright you pain."

Suvi-jean furrowed her brow and gave Amanda a puzzled look. "How do you mean? Mandy, I don't believe you would ever bring me pain, not deliberately. I don't understand."

Amanda sighed and looked away, still blushing. "I'm just afraid that I might say or do something that you could misinterpret and ... ah crap, I'm messing this up. I ..."

"You're afraid I'll ask you for sex." Suvi-jean chuckled at the shocked look on Amanda's face. "Relax, my friend, that's the last thing in this lifetime I'd be interested in."

"Jeannie?"

"I've been forced to have sex far too often. No, I've had enough sex pain for a lifetime. Amanda, I'll speak plainly with you, I do have needs,

needs that have never been met, but I hoped that, in time, we could become close enough for that to happen for me."

"Wait, pain? You find sex painful? You were forced?"

"Yes to all the above, I was slave, remember?"

"Oh gods, Jeannie, I'm so sorry all that happened to you. Honey, you said you have needs, may I ask what they are?"

"I ache inside for closeness, the gentle loving touch of another person. When I was a child the captain used to play chase the ball with me. It was only for a few stolen moments, but at the end he always patted my shoulder and told me I was a good girl. That touch, it was so magical, it held warmth. No one else ever touched me with such affection. He really liked me, and I could tell."

"No one? Not even your mother?"

"No, not even. Had I been a super-lightspeed engine, maybe, but I was merely something that tore her away from her work. Loving human touch, that's what I crave. I go to sleep fantasizing about being cuddled in the arms of someone who genuinely likes me."

"By all that's holy, I can make that happen for you right now. Scooch over." Amanda hopped over to the big chair Suvi-jean was in and squeezed in beside her. "Trust me, I won't hurt you. Just relax into my arms now, rest your head on my shoulder."

She kissed the top of Suvi-jean's head as the girl settled down against her. Suvi-jean was a bit stiff at first, but all too soon the tears started to flow, followed by great heaving sobs that racked her body. Amanda held her tight and rocked her as the storm of pent up emotions escaped Suvi-jean's iron control.

When the storm had passed, and she lay quietly in Amanda's arms, Amanda kissed her hair again. "Honey, when was the last time you had a good cry?"

"Over seventeen years ago, the day they put the pain collar on me and demonstrated its effects."

Amanda hugged her tightly again. "Well then, you were long past due." Suvi-jean started to untangle herself and sit back up, but Amanda pulled her back down onto her shoulder. "Oh no, Missy, you're not getting away yet. I'm not done hugging you."

Her hug was enthusiastically returned. Soon the tears started again, but more softly this time. Amanda rocked her gently and held her until Suvi-jean cried herself to sleep.

Chapter #5

A New Day

Suvi-jean awakened to the alarm. It took a moment to understand she wasn't alone, she was in her bed entangled in Amanda's arms. Amanda groaned and sat up. "Hey there."

"Hi."

"Jeannie, are you okay?"

"I feel light inside, as though something has been taken away. What did you do to me?"

"You were hurting, honey. I held you while you cried yourself to sleep then tucked you in. It's what best friends do."

"Best friends? Are we that, Amanda? Please, can we be?"

"Yeah, I think that's what we are, Jeannie. Listen you, next time I come apart I'll be expecting you to keep me safe."

"Amanda, you know I will. Yes, that's it, that's what happened. You held me, and I felt safe. It was so new, different, and it loosened something inside me. I can never thank you enough for that."

"Look, I know there'll be more of this for you. There will, until you release all the pain and fear from the past, all the hurt. I'll always be here for you when you need to release. I promise."

Amanda saw the adoration in the girl's eyes and sighed. She pulled her close and kissed her forehead. "Now, I have to scoot to my quarters, get a shower and a fresh uniform. You do the same and I'll meet you in the mess, okay?"

"Okay. Mandy, I ..."

"Hush. Get in the shower now." Amanda fled Suvi-jean's quarters and hurried to her own. "Dammit, Mandy, you might have stepped in it this time," she admonished herself. "You've got to be careful here. This woman is a savage alien warrior, and a frightened little girl at the same time. She has no real experience, no filters at all, and has never known a single kindness in her entire life."

Donning a fresh uniform, she raced to the mess, grabbed a cup of coffee and a sandwich then took it to the table where her three friends were waiting. "So, spent the night at your girlfriend's?" said Jake.

Amanda slammed her plate on the table. "Listen up, all three of you. Suvi-jean may be the crazy alien warrior with super powers who can kill us all in a heartbeat, and she is all of that, but she's also been a slave all her life, used and abused at every turn. She needs patience and understanding while she learns how to be human, learns about emotions, social mores, and the rest. You three will be gentle with, and kind to, her while she works through it all, or I'll personally spill your guts on the deck. Understand?" She was glaring right at Jake.

"Understood," he said, holding up his hands defensively.

"I mean it, Jake."

"I know, Mandy, I know. I saw that yesterday. Suvi-jean was really trying, and she didn't have to. We'll do what we can to help her. I swear it."

"Jake, I'm warning you, don't make a pass at her."

"What???"

"Jake, she grew up a slave, think about what that means."

"Yeah, but ... Oh crap, you mean she was ..."

"Yes."

"Well fuck, that's just ugly. Okay, got it. Suvi-jean is officially the table's little sister, right guys?"

Carla and Hal agreed. "Here she comes now," said Carla. "Hi Suvi-jean."

"Hello friendly people. How is everyone today?"

"We're good. So, how're you doing? Ow!"

"Jake, before you start work today I suggest you stop by the armory and requisition some leg armor before Carla gives you a permanent injury." That brought a round of chuckles. "Carla, it's okay; I know Jake was just teasing. It's okay. He waved at me when he saw Amanda leaving my quarters this morning."

"Oh, okay," said Carla, blushing slightly.

"So, what was that all about?" asked Jake, swiftly swinging his long legs out of the line of fire.

"Wouldn't you like to know?" replied Suvi-jean.

"Oh yeah," he smirked, leaning closer to her, "I sure would." Both Carla and Amanda looked ready to shoot him, but Suvi-jean just grinned. "Life's so full of disappointments, Jake."

"And that's on the list?"

"Right at the top."

Jake laughed heartily. "Suvi-jean, I think you'll do. Friends?"

He offered his hand and she shook it. "Friends, Jake. "That gentle loving way you have with people will be a great help to me."

"Well done, Jeannie," he grinned. "You understand the concept and application of sarcasm already."

"My mother would be proud of me." He gave her a questioning look, so she went on. "One of the changes the virus made in me was to give me full genetic memory. I focused on my mother and her manner of handling social interaction, knowing you would tease me about Amanda. Mom was great at sarcasm. So, how did I do?"

"Awesome. I'm humbled by your powers. Full genetic memory? Really?"

She nodded. "Yep, really."

"Dang, that could be handy." Again she nodded. He laughed and gave her a warm smile. "Have a great day, Ensign Sorenson. I'll look forward to your visit." He stood and walked away with that odd form of locomotion that was unique to him.

"He has a most interesting way of walking," mused Suvi-jean.

"You mean he walks funny," grinned Carla.

"No, seriously," said Suvi-jean. "His upper body is completely at rest. It's most efficient."

"And funny."

"Yes, Carla, definitely funny," grinned Suvi-jean. "So, Hal, how are the bruises?"

"They're turning all sorts of pretty colors, want to see?"

"I'll take your word for it," she said, matching his grin.

"What's on your list of fun things for today, Jeannie?" asked Carla.

"I thought I'd pay a visit to you at the infirmary, and then go see what Jake's up to. Hal, can you tell me, no, wait, I'll ask him myself."

"What? What is it Suvi-jean? Is it Jake? He doesn't mean any harm. Honest."

"I know. However, I sense a deep bitterness in him, and I wonder why. It's okay, I'll wait until he's more comfortable with me then ask him about it."

"It's no big secret, Jeannie," said Amanda. "In the beginning there were five ships like this one. When they returned to Earth for more settlers they found the planet destroyed by war. The captains of the ships got together and decided to scrap four of them and make one load of settlers from the combined crews."

"And?"

"And, as hard as they searched they weren't able to find a likely planet to colonize. Desperate, Captain Baris brought us back here, hoping we could join your colony. Now it looks like we'll have to continue the search for a new home."

Suvi-jean nodded at this, absorbing the information and its implications. "All right, I understand. So where does Jake fit into this, and how has this made him, in particular, bitter?"

"Like you, I was born on this ship," replied Amanda, "but Jake and Hal weren't. Jake and Hal were both trained for security, but when the crews were blended, there weren't enough positions."

"So Jake wound up in Sanitation."

"Yes, he's applied for a transfer a dozen times over the past eight years, but we're the young blood," said Hal.

"And with the blending of five crews there were plenty of senior people to choose from," said Suvi-jean, nodding her head. "Got it."

"Jeannie honey, what's going through that mind of yours?"

"Why, Mandy, what makes you think ..."

Amanda laughed. "I know you, Suvi-jean. That mind of yours never stops. What are you thinking?"

"I think I need to have a chat with the chief engineer and the captain." She rose lightly to her feet and smiling, strode away. "Have a wonderful day, my friends."

"What just happened?" asked Carla.

"I think somebody just had an idea, and I think Jake's life will soon become far more interesting," grinned Amanda. "Okay, I'm off to work. Later guys."

Chapter #6

Showdown

Suvi-jean stopped off at the infirmary on her way to Sanitation. She was met by the Chief of staff, Dr. Eamon Reilly. "Good morning, Suvi-jean. What brings you here, are you ready for a full examination?"

"No, Dr. Reilly, but I brought you something," she said as she held up a small leather pouch. He gave her a puzzled look, so she smiled and went on. "The berries that neutralized the virus in me. I had some with me. I thought you might want to check out their properties in case they might be useful against other things. There's a few seeds as well, it might be possible to grow some as an addition to the general food source."

"Oh lord, yes, I'd love to have a look at those. Thank you, Suvi-jean. Now, Carla said to expect you today, but I thought you were working on getting the Security forces in readiness."

"That is my main task, and will remain so until this is resolved, but, sadly, I fear this department will be extremely busy very soon. If I'm wrong, then no harm done, but ..."

"Yes, I agree, and we've been preparing. I'll let Carla fill you in, show you around, while I go play with the new toys you brought me." He gestured with his hand and Carla stepped forward. Together she and Suvi-jean watched him hurry into the lab.

Carla smiled and led Suvi-jean through the facility. It had originally been built to serve over twelve thousand crew and passengers, so now only half was normally kept open. However, in anticipation of possible casualties, the full facility was open and ready. Commander Reilly had also brought on extra staff.

"This is wonderful, Carla," said Suvi-jean. "You people have done well. I'll have good things to tell the captain about this department."

Carla beamed her pleasure at that. "Jeannie, are you going to visit Jake today too?"

"Yes, Sanitation is my next stop. You're worried about him?"

"Yeah, I guess I am. He's tried so hard for so long to get out of there, and it's killing him. I can see him slipping into depression again and I'm afraid this time, oh I just …"

"You have a special liking for Jake, yes?"

"What, no, I just …" Carla was blushing furiously. "Listen you, don't you dare say a word to him or …"

"Fear not, friend Carla," grinned Suvi-jean, "I have enough scars, and Jake signed out the last pair of shin armament."

"What??? Why you … beast, you're an alien beast. Gods, just look at me blush. Jeannie Sorenson, you're bad."

"I'm sorry, Carla. I was only playing, are you truly angry? I didn't mean to offend you, I …"

Suddenly Carla remembered what Amanda had said. "No, Jeannie, I'm just playing too, I'm not offended. A little embarrassed, but not offended. It's okay."

"You truly don't want anyone to know of your feelings for Jake?"

"No."

"Why not?"

"Because we're all friends, and if he doesn't return my feelings, which he probably doesn't, it would make things extremely awkward for everybody."

"Are you sure he doesn't share your feelings?"

"I'm pretty sure. He's too infatuated with the new Ensign."

"New Ensign?"

"You."

"Me?"

"Oh don't play the innocent, you … Jeannie, you really couldn't tell?"

"No. Carla, I call on the experiences and behaviors of my predecessors for social interactions, but I have little or no true understanding of what any of it really means."

"Oh, Jeannie, I'm so sorry."

"Does he ...?"

"He does."

"This cannot ever be. Carla, trust me when I say, that cannot ever be. What should I do?"

"Just be yourself, Suvi-jean, he'll get over it in time. Mandy has already warned him off."

"Mandy?"

"She's very protective of you."

"She is a wonderful friend. Carla, if you think it would be helpful, I'll see about getting Jake out of Sanitation and into another job."

"Oh my god, Jeannie, can you do that?"

"I can certainly try. That's what friends do, isn't it? They try to make life better for each other?"

"Indeed they do, my friend. Indeed they do."

"This is all so new and exciting for me."

"Oh?"

"I've never had friends before, Carla. Not ever. This being free to choose my own path, share time with people who like me just for me, it's all quite heady stuff." Carla smiled and gave her arm a gentle squeeze. "I'll head on down to Sanitation now. I'll put some thought into what to do with our friend down there."

With that she turned and headed out the door. Carla sighed and smiled as she watched her go. She'd originally been afraid of this alien woman, but the more she got to know her the more she saw the innocent and frightened child inside. Amanda had been right, they needed to be careful and gentle with Suvi-jean.

As Suvi-jean entered the Sanitation department the supervisor wasn't in the office. Suvi-jean pushed open the door that said authorized personnel only beyond this point. Stepping through several things assaulted her senses at the same time. There were angry raised voices and a terrible stench. There stood Jake, covered in something vile, and a large man in a starched uniform shouting at him.

"Crewman White, what the hell have you done this time?"

"I changed out that suction valve, Supervisor Ellay."

"And just who authorized you to do that?"

"No one."

"Excuse me, Crewman White?"

"No one authorized the change out, Supervisor Ellay."

"So you took it upon yourself to waste the ship's resources?" Jake didn't respond. "Well?"

"Look, I've had to crawl into the shit and sludge six times in the last month to clear that valve. It had to be replaced and you know it."

"I'm putting you on report for insubordination and theft."

"Theft?"

"You removed an intake valve from stores without authorization, that's theft and you know it. You're finished this time, White. I'll see you in the brig for this."

"Excuse me," said Suvi-jean, "but I fail to see why a man doing his job is cause for punishment?"

The big man turned to face Suvi-jean. "How did you get in here?"

"Through that door."

"You're not authorized to be in here, Ensign. Get out before I put you on report too."

"My name is Ensign Suvi-jean Sorenson, and by order of the captain, I'm authorized to go wherever I please on this ship. I repeat, why is a man doing his job cause for punishment?"

"I don't care who the hell you are, Ensign. This is my department; I say who comes and goes here. Now get out." He took a step into her personal space and glowered down at her. "Get moving, that's an order."

The man went into shock as steely fingers grasped his throat, chocking off his air supply and lifting him off his feet. "My days as a slave are over," she snarled. "No one orders me now."

Jake was suddenly beside her, pressing down on her arm. "Easy, Jeannie, easy. Let him go now, let him go. He's not worth the trouble, girl, he's not." She thrust the man away and he stood fearfully, holding his throat, and coughing as he dragged great lungsful of air back into his body.

"Jake?"

"It's okay, Jeannie, it s okay. You go on now, I'll deal with this."

"I don't think it's safe to leave you alone with this man. He wants to attack you."

"I know, Jeannie, I know. I'll be fine. If he tries anything I'll drown him in that cesspool I just crawled out of, and say he fell in by accident. I'll be safe."

"Are you sure?"

He gave her a sloppy grin. "Go on now, I got this."

She gazed into his eyes for a moment. "Be patient, Jake. I will get you out of here." With that she turned on her heel and left.

Jake turned to the supervisor. "I wasn't joking about drowning you, you fucking moron. I just saved your life, you owe me, so listen up. That woman is Ensign Sorenson, the captain's eyes and ears on the ship. She's also an alien warrior. You give her attitude like that again and she's crack your skull like an eggshell.

"The captain gave her free run of the ship, she looks for weaknesses, inefficiencies, and anything else that strikes her fancy, and then reports back to him. She's also a special favorite of Commander Hoffman. You make trouble for her and Hoffman will be all over you like a bad rash.

"Now, you do whatever you like to me, because I really don't give a sweet fuck anymore. No matter what happens, it can't get any worse than working for you in this shit hole. You mess with Suvi-jean, she'll finish you."

"Fuck you, White. Regulations are regulations, even the captain can't change that. You're going on report and so is that savage."

With that he stalked away. Jake sighed and wiped some of the sewage off his face. "Aw, crap, that asshole is going to make a fuss over this. I'll do my best to take the heat for it, I just hope the captain isn't too pissed. Maybe I should drown the shithead. God, Mandy's going to kill me for getting her in trouble." With another sigh he headed for the showers.

While Jake stood under the cascading water, trying to get the sludge out of his hair, Suvi-jean was in Security. "You sure about this, Suvi-jean?"

"Yes, Commander, I'm sure. Mr. White was completely professional as he de-escalated the situation, separated the combatants, and encouraged me to leave the area to ensure no further hostilities."

"Here's his file, it says pretty clearly that this man has a serious attitude problem, resents authority, and ..."

"And every complaint on that file was registered by Supervisor Ellay."

"Well I'll be damned, you're right there. So you're saying this supervisor is the one with the problem."

"I'm saying Jake has security training, and this man seems to have a grudge, is deliberately holding him back. For the immediate future we need more security men, he has the training, and he's motivated. Can't we give him a chance?"

"You called him by his first name, friend of yours?" grinned Brandon Hoffman.

"We met in the mess. He's an odd character all right, but yes, I think I could call him a friend, at least I hope to one day."

Commander Hoffman gazed into her eyes for a moment and realized she had no idea he was teasing her or how. He relented. "All right, Suvi-jean, I'll sign the transfer. Put him where you want him."

"I think the infirmary. We could have lots of action there once the worst is over, some may not be our people. I think the presence of a security man there could go a long way to keeping a lid on things."

He slowly nodded his agreement. Yes, she was trying to help a friend, but she was also still holding the big picture in mind, keeping the newbie out of the real action. "Okay, Ensign Sorenson, here's his transfer chip, put him where you want him."

"Shift's nearly over," she smiled brightly. "I'll see if I can catch him in the mess."

As Suvi-jean hurried away, Brandon Hoffman noticed the look he was getting from his second in command. "Problem, Sub-commander Singh?"

"No sir," she grinned in reply.

"But?"

"But that's the first time I've ever seen you do a favor for any subordinate, ever."

"She's not my subordinate, she works for the captain."

"So, your record's still intact?"

"Yup. I don't know, Sheila, there's just something about her, the way her mind works. It's like two people thinking at once. She wanted to help her friend, but she also searched out his record and caught the one thing I hadn't actually noticed before. I think this young fellow may have been getting a raw deal, and we need all the highly motivated officers we can get."

"I think she reminds you of somebody you once knew, and that's a good thing."

"It is?"

"Proves you're still human. Go home, it's my shift now anyway." Chuckling he grinned and walked away.

Chapter #7

In Trouble

Jake was just coming out of the Sanitation station when the announcement came. "Crewman Jakob White, Ensign Suvi-jean Sorenson, and Supervisor Carl Ellay to the First Officer's meeting room."

"Well shit," grumbled Jake, "I really should have drowned that fat bastard. If Suvi-jean's in trouble for this I swear I will."

The three of them arrived and stood at attention while First Officer Olga Volkov studied her screen. Dr. Reilly was also there, sitting relaxed in a chair. Finally she looked up from her desk and spoke.

"I have several complaints here. We shall address them one at a time. First, Crewman White, you stand accused of theft from ship's stores and insubordination. How do you plead?"

"Guilty, Ma'am."

"Guilty? Have you anything to say in your defense?"

"Ma'am there's an intake valve in the sewage area that should have been replaced months ago. It continued to get worse and needed repairs more often. I took a new valve from stores and installed it against the wishes of my supervisor."

"You're certain your supervisor wouldn't approve the change."

"Yes Ma'am, I am."

"Supervisor Ellay, what do you have to say to this? Did you indeed refuse to allow the replacement of the defective valve?"

"In my opinion it would have lasted longer. I don't believe in wasting the ship's resources."

"So, you deliberately withheld the replacement of a sewage valve," said Dr. Reilly, "all the while knowing full well you were exposing this man and others to dangerous bacteria. Good Christ, you could have started an epidemic throughout the ship. Good sanitation is of the utmost importance, it's vital to the survival of this crew."

The first officer leaned across her desk. "Mr. Ellay, you are hereby reduced in rank to spaceman third class. You will continue to work in the sanitation department, but under close supervision. Report for duty tomorrow as usual, your new supervisor will be there waiting. Dismissed."

"But what about the other charges ...?"

"They will be dealt with right now," replied the first officer. "You are dismissed, Mr. Ellay." Shaken and beaten, he turned and left the office.

"Now, Mr. White. I don't believe you should remain in Sanitation. I have here a report that you witnessed an altercation there today, that you expertly intervened, separated the combatants, and de-escalated the situation. This, plus the initiative shown by recognizing the danger to ship's crew, and taking steps to counteract that threat, tells me your skills can be better used elsewhere.

"Mr. Jakob White, you are now promoted to spaceman first class and reassigned to Security on a temporary basis until we find a better fit for your skills. Report to Security in the morning to get your uniform and assignment. Dismissed."

Stunned, Jake just stood there, his mouth open. "Dismissed, Mr. White," grinned the first officer.

Finally Jake found his voice. "Yes ma'am, thank you, ma'am." He turned and left her office.

Once Jake had shut the door Olga turned to Suvi-jean. "And now for you. You stand accused of choking a crewman of lesser rank, how do you plead?"

"Guilty."

Olga chuckled as did the doctor. "Suvi-jean, I'm not doubting that fool deserved it, but why?"

"He stepped close, threateningly, and commanded me to leave. His tone and posture were that of a master speaking to a slave, and it triggered a level of defiance in me that demanded action. I am slave no longer. I no longer have to be spoken to like that and cower in fear."

"Suvi-jean, girl, you can't beat up all the assholes on the entire ship," sighed Olga. "If you do we'll be extremely short handed. Look, I know you're trying to find your way, and I'll help you all I can, but I do have to put a reprimand on your record."

"What will it say?"

Startled, Olga looked up and saw the face of a child who unwittingly had found herself in trouble. She melted inside. "It will say, Ensign Sorenson was accused and pled guilty to using excess force to subdue an aggressive crewman. It's not so bad really, Suvi-jean. Most of the Security guys have at least two or more of these on their record. Brandon has eight, I think."

"So, it won't impede my ability to do my job?"

"No girl, not a bit. Look, I understand, I do. Just keep in mind, no matter how ignorant and aggressive they get, they dare not touch you, and if they do then you can kick the crap out of them in self-defence."

Suvi-jean looked thoughtful. "This learning to be fully human is a lot harder than I imagined it would be." This made both officers chuckle. "I'd like to point out one thing. Mr. White was far more provoked than I was, but he managed to hold himself in check. Perhaps I should ask him for advice about this."

"Not a bad idea at that," smiled Olga Volkov. "Now, the captain wants to see you, Suvi-jean. Off you go."

She saluted and left the office, turning the corner to enter the captain's meeting room. "You wanted to see me, Captain Baris? Am I in trouble? Please don't put me off the ship."

"What??? No, Jeannie, girl, you're not in trouble. I know about that mess today. The man's an idiot. Look, part of this is my fault. I made you an Ensign, but I can see that still allows some crew to disrespect you. That man should never have spoken to you as he did. I hereby promote you to Sub-commander."

He made a note on his official log then looked up. "Now, here's why I wanted to see you. Brandon thinks we're as ready as we can be to face the grounders. I wanted to get your assessment before I sent the invitation to the First Prime. Are we ready, Jeannie?"

"Commander Hoffman's correct, we should do this as soon as possible while everyone is still alert and ready for it. The longer we wait now, the more lax our own people will become."

"I like the way your mind works, Jeannie. All right, first thing in the morning put everybody on full alert. I'll contact Farouk and invite him up. Get some rest, Jeannie, tomorrow will be an exciting day."

Chapter #8

Invasion

Her three friends were waiting for her when Suvi-jean arrived at the mess hall. Jake stood up and stepped toward her. "Woman, you're a goddess, and I'll worship you forever for what you've done. Please tell me I can pick you up, twirl you around, and hug you, just this once."

She tilted her head sideways and looked at him. "You're serious?"

"I sure am."

"Have you ever done this to another?"

"Both Carla and Mandy in the past ten minutes."

"So, it's a ritual of pleasure?" He nodded his head, a grin starting to form on his lips. "Okay, then, do it."

With a shout of joy Jake swept her into his arms and pulled her off her feet, swinging her around and around. A shriek of surprised laughter escaped her lips as she sped through the air. He set her gently on her feet and kissed the top of her head. "Suvi-jean, I love you."

She gently placed her hands on his chest and stepped back. "So, you're happy?" she smiled.

"Beyond expression, beyond belief."

"Then I'm happy, Jake. Let's sit down now, I'm hungry."

They sat then he spoke again. "I expected to end up in the brig, but I got my transfer and a promotion. Jeannie, what did they do to you?"

"The first officer put a reprimand on my record."

"Ouch," said Amanda.

"Not to fret, Mandy, she said all the security people have at least two or more. Then the captain wanted to see me. He gave me a promotion to Sub-Commander, so crewmen won't be so quick to disrespect me, and said tomorrow's the big day. He's going to invite the First Prime to the ship, so I'll either be proved wrong, or all hell will break loose."

"Wow," said Amanda. "You've had a busy day. Are you okay?"

"I'm a little nervous about tomorrow. If I'm right a lot of good people will get hurt before it's over. If I'm wrong a lot of people will be angry with me, and no one will ever trust me again."

"Aw honey, want company tonight?"

"Yes please. This is all so strange for me."

"Oh?"

"Yes. Normally, I wouldn't care about it one way or the other, in fact I liked people not trusting me, fearing me, and I was always confident in my intuitions, but now I really want people to trust me, my instincts, and that makes me doubt myself, makes me vulnerable."

Hal leaned his elbows on the table and spoke softly. "Jeannie, how often are your instincts wrong?"

"They haven't been yet. I always know when danger is coming, and right now I know it's nearly upon us."

"That's good enough for me. So, any idea where they plan to station old Jake?"

"The infirmary." Carla's eyes opened wide and she stared at Suvi-jean. "We need our experienced people at the incursion points, but I expect lots of action at the infirmary once things get going. Today Jake demonstrated he has the skills to keep things from getting out of hand, but he's a bit rusty for the front lines. I thought this would be a good way for him to ease into the job." Under the table Carla gave Suvi-jean's hand a tight squeeze.

"Sounds perfect," grinned Jake, winking at Carla to make her blush. "First Officer Volkov said this was a temporary posting. Do you ...?"

Suvi-jean reached across the table to lightly grip his arm for a moment. "Jake, trust me and be patient. I swear I'll do everything in my power to keep you out of that old job. Just be patient and trust me."

He started to say something sarcastic, but stopped himself. He could see the earnestness in her eyes. "All right, Jeannie, I'll leave it up to you. You've been damn good to me so far."

"So, how does freedom feel, Jake?" asked Amanda.

"Awesome, Mandy. God, I was ready for, and actually looking forward to, a stint in the brig. At least in there I wouldn't have to crawl through crap, or listen to Ellay whine. Instead, I get the job I always wanted, and a promotion to boot. It's downright euphoric."

"Well, people, it's time for rest," said Amanda as she rose to her feet and took Suvi-jean by the hand. "Tomorrow's going to be an exciting day."

* * * * *

"Mandy, are you okay?" asked Suvi-jean as they settled down with refreshments.

"Huh? Oh, sure, I'm fine. Like you I'm a bit nervous about tomorrow. I'm in command of transport after all."

"I honestly believe they'll use their own transport system. That way they can pinpoint their targets more easily. I don't think they ..."

"They could hijack our system. If it's turned on they can hijack the beam and use that as well."

"Oh crap. I didn't know that, Mandy. I should send those Security men back to you."

"No, no, honey, I have a plan. I'll be watching and the instant I see a flicker I'll shut our beam down."

"That will kill whoever is in transit."

"Yes it will, and that's the plan. Oh Jeannie, I'm sorry. Please don't think I'm a heartless bloodthirsty savage. I'm just terrified of ..."

Suvi-jean was on her feet with Amanda in her arms in a heartbeat. "No, Mandy, no. I don't think anything like that. I think you're brave, strong, smart, bewitchingly beautiful, intoxicatingly divine to feel in my arms, and ..."

Amanda burst out laughing. "Suvi-jean Sorenson, you're wicked, and you know that flattery will get you everywhere." She hugged Suvi-jean tightly.

"Will it get you to stay the night and snuggle with me?"

"Yes it will, sweetheart. Yes it will."

Suvi-jean leaned back a bit to gaze into Amanda's eyes. "Sweetheart is a special endearment or an insult depending on how it's spoken, yes?"

"Yes, it is," replied Amanda. "Jeannie, I ..."

"I don't believe you wanted to insult me. Does this mean you want us to be special best friends, lovers?"

"Honey, I know you don't want anything to do with sex. I get that. However, I get the sense you want a special bond with me, and I'll freely admit, I like that idea, I want that too. Would you like to try it for a while to see if it will work for you?"

"Oh, Mandy, the idea scares me, but I want it, I do. I don't know how to do this. Will you teach me?"

"Well, for starters, we do lots of this hugging thing when we're alone. We share things about our day, our jobs, the people we work with, our hopes and dreams, we snuggle, we spend time alone, and when we're with friends we stay close to each other, so others know we're bonding. Does any of this work for you?"

"All of it, Mandy. All of it, but I'm afraid I'll do something wrong and embarrass you or make you angry."

"We'll go slow, carefully, take our time as we test the waters."

"You promise?"

"I promise, but you'll have to flatter me a lot."

"It will be my undying pleasure to compliment you constantly, my delight, my precious girl. Is it okay to call you my girlfriend?"

"Yes, it is, honey. I like the title. You can call me sweetheart too if you want."

"I do want to, sweetheart," smiled Suvi-jean, "and each time I do, it will always be a term of endearment." She pulled Amanda closer, hugging her tightly again.

"Suvi-jean."

"I know, not when we're on duty. Mandy, this won't make you look bad to the other officers, will it? You being an Ensign and me being a Sub-commander."

"No, honey, it won't, just don't get too bossy."

"I won't, I promise, and if I do you can remind me of the promise."

"Sweetheart, my precious Jeannie, I was teasing."

"Oh. Damn. I missed the cue again. I'll get the hang of it, Mandy, I will."

"I know you will, honey. I know you will. Come on now, time for bed. Let's go wash up."

They crawled into the bed and Amanda held Suvi-jean and rocked her to sleep. "Well that worked, Amanda," she thought to herself as she kissed the top of Suvi-jean's head. "You got her mind off the coming battle so she wouldn't get overcome with nerves, but you moved the relationship thing along a lot faster than you'd planned."

She placed another kiss on the girl's head and smiled softly. "She doesn't seem to mind though."

* * * * *

They walked hand in hand to the mess hall, gathered their breakfasts then sat side by side. Hal looked at them and grinned. "Hmm, I see something's changed overnight."

"Shut up, Hal," growled Amanda as she took a long sip of her coffee. Suvi-jean stiffened so Amanda relented. "Easy, sweetheart, Hal was just teasing."

"Oh, then I don't have to choke him out?"

"No, honey, ..."

"Easy, sweetheart, I was teasing too, at least I was trying to. Sorry Hal, I guess I still need to work on it."

"I don't know," grinned Jake, "I liked it."

Amanda gripped Suvi-jean's hand tightly. "Honey, I'm so sorry. You were teasing, and I didn't catch it. This one was my ..."

Before she could finish her sentence Suvi-jean leaped to her feet, the look of the warrior in her eyes as they turned amber. "Shit, it's happening now. Battle stations!"

She fled the mess, leaving the others staring open mouthed at each other. As she vanished through the archway the captain's voice sounded over the ship's speakers. "Battle stations, battle stations, this is not a drill. Battle stations, senior staff to the bridge."

The captain was still giving his announcement as Suvi-jean came racing down the corridor towards the air filtration station. Half her troops were already there, and the rest were coming. "Fire. Fire the gas canisters now. Fire." Several looked stunned, but three fired.

It was lucky they did. In a flash of light sixteen SUVI appeared. Suvi-jean had her gas filter on her face and was firing her stun gun as she charged into their midst. "Fire. Keep Firing."

The SUVI reacted, but it was too late. In their moment of arrival that first breath had dosed them with enough knockout gas to slow them down. As soon as they appeared the human troops opened fire with the stunners. Suvi-jean was the only one wearing a stun shield and so was the only one unaffected. Within moments the SUVI were down and in restraints.

The air cleansing system soon sucked out the gas and Suvi-jean tossed aside her mask. "Quickly now, they won't be out for long. Let's get them into the brig." An inter ship transport was initiated and they all suddenly appeared beside the cells. The SUVI were dragged into cells and locked inside. They were starting to revive.

Suvi-jean watched one man in particular for a moment. He groaned and rolled to his feet, looking at his bound hand with a puzzled expression. "SUVI 13, are you functional?"

"What? Oh, yes, ... SUVI 5, is that you? You escaped the collar? What happened to us?" The others were awake now to one degree or another.

"I will explain. I'm no longer SUVI 5, I am now Suvi-jean Sorenson. You were hit with stun gas and placed under arrest. SUVI 13, do you trust me?"

"Of course he does," came another voice, "we all do. What's going to happen to us?"

"You will not be harmed. It's my plan to get those collars off you and then the captain will decide what happens next. Will you hold still and not attack me while I remove your collars?"

Number thirteen stepped closer to the bars. "We trust you, you're the one who freed our minds. I'll be still as stone if you want to set my body free as well."

"Open the cell."

"Ma'am ..."

"Trust me, it's all right. Open the cell."

"Yes, ma'am." The crewman flicked a switch and the cell door slid open. Suvi-jean stepped inside carrying heavy bolt cutters. She cut the pain collar off the man then cut the bonds from his wrists. "Wait here until I come back for you." She stepped to the next SUVI.

* * * * *

Cursing like a madman, Hal hid behind his shield. "I can't believe those bastards are using live projectiles inside a spaceship. Are they trying to blow the hull?"

"Squad leader, what do we do? We can't fight them with just stunners, they ..."

"Pull back."

"Squad leader?"

"I said pull back. I'll get a couple of stun grenades into them then you can haul them off to the brig."

"You can't ... you'll be caught in ..."

"Shut up and pull back." Hal suddenly broke from cover, running zig-zag down the wide corridor. Several bullets tore into his body, but he threw the grenades as he fell. He'd already pulled the pins. Within moments the attackers were on their way to the brig and Hal was on the way to the infirmary. Suvi-jean arrived as they took him away.

She got a quick report from a crewman then bolted for the transportation room. She met Amanda coming out with a small man in custody. "You?"

"Good to see you again, Second Prime." She grabbed him by the collar and dragged him toward the bridge.

On the bridge they found a standoff. Farouk Bladon was there with SUVI 19 at his side. There were also several more men with weapons pointed at the bridge crew, but the crew was armed and pointing back. "Captain, this is futile," said Farouk. "My people have already taken the ship. Surrender and no harm will befall you. Resist me and I'll have to kill the lot of you."

"You're mistaken," said a harsh voice behind him.

Farouk Bladon spun around to see Suvi-jean, her eyes glowing amber, holding the Second Prime by the collar. "You. You're dead."

"SUVI 5 is dead. I'm Suvi-jean Sorenson, and I'm very much alive." She shoved the Second Prime at Amanda. "Ensign Drake, if this one moves, kill it." Amanda took the man by the collar and hauled him aside where he stood trembling in fear.

"Farouk Bladon, your forces have failed. The SUVI are in the brig as are many more of the humans you beamed to this ship, at least two dozed are dead, the rest defeated."

"SUVI 5, you've disappointed me for the last time. Nineteen, kill that traitor."

Two wicked looking blades leaped to the hands of SUVI 19 as he locked eyes with Suvi-jean. His arm flashed and there was a soft thud, then Farouk Bladon's smile changed to a look of shock. His eyes wandered down to the knife hilt protruding from his chest. With a half step forward, he turned his gaze on SUVI 19.

The next blow was savage, driven by a powerful arm as SUVI 19 buried the second blade in Farouk Bladon's chest. As Farouk sank to the floor lifeless, Suvi-jean stepped up to SUVI 19. "Be still a moment."

She seized the collar around his neck and heaved. The metal snapped, and she cast aside the collar then stepped back. "Together?"

"As needed," he replied.

He put his back to hers as she turned to the armed men and spoke. "The SUVI have been captured, your master is dead. Surrender now and live, refuse and Nineteen and I will kill the lot of you. ... Drop your weapons, now." Slowly they obeyed. SUVI 19 gathered up the weapons and set them aside out of reach.

Suvi-jean turned to the captain. "Captain Baris, the ship is secure."

"Excellent work, Commander Sorenson. Security Chief, have these men removed to the brig. Commander Sorenson, report."

"The SUVI were captured without incident, captain. The three other incursion points were successfully defended, but several were killed on both sides plus there are many wounded on both sides. I have no accurate numbers at this time.

"Once I was assured they were defeated I hurried here. I found Ensign Drake with her captive by the door, the rest you know."

"Thank you, Commander Sorenson. Chief of Security, report."

"Sir. Thanks to Commander Sorenson's warning, we were prepared for the attempted takeover of the ship. My people are mopping up things now, getting the able captives to the brig, taking the rest to the infirmary or the morgue. I have three squads hunting through the ship for any strays that might have been missed, and I'm keeping guards on all ship's systems until I'm convinced we're clear."

"Excellent. All right people, make sure the ship is clear, see to all necessary repairs, then report back to me. Commander Sorenson, Sub-Commander Drake, congratulations on your battlefield promotions."

"Thank you, sir."

The captain grinned. "Jeannie, how did you manage to capture the SUVI without a casualty?"

"I sensed them coming, Captain. I ran to my station and arrived in time to fire the knockout gas before they landed. They appeared into a cloud of it, and we hit them with stunners. It was the timing. Had I been a few minutes slower they'd have been loose in the ship. We were lucky, as they were vital to the attack plan. Without the SUVI the invaders had no chance for success."

"And they're all in the brig?"

"Yes Sir. I removed their slave collars then asked them to remain there until you could decide what to do next."

The captain nodded. "What do you suggest I do with then, Jeannie?"

"Sir, could we ask them what they'd like to do?"

Again he nodded. "Very well then, take this man down to join them, and see what they'd like to do. You and I'll confer first thing tomorrow and go from there."

"Aye, Sir." Suvi-jean turned and led Nineteen away.

The Captain grinned at Amanda. "You're curious why I promoted you."

"Forgive me, Captain, but, yes, I am curious."

"Remember your specialized training."

"Of course, I ... Wait, do you mean ...?"

"I do. Go assign someone else to transportation, then open up the Social Engagement office, dust it off, and assume the post. First Officer Volkov will assign personnel to your staff tomorrow."

With a huge grin of delight Amanda snapped off a salute and fled the bridge.

Chapter #9

After the Battle

The next day the breakfast meeting was quite subdued. Amanda had spent the night with Suvi-jean once again and they arrived together, hand in hand. Jake noticed and winked at Carla who blushed and swatted his arm.

"Looks like we won, Jeannie," said Jake as she and Amanda brought their food to the table.

"We did, but there were casualties. I saw Hal being taken to the infirmary. Did he survive?"

"He did," said Carla. "He'll be laid up for a while, but he'll make a full recovery."

"What exactly happened there?" asked Amanda.

"The report says he saved all his people," replied Suvi-jean. "They were losing, being pushed back, when Hal suddenly carried two gas grenades into enemy forces. He took several wounds but managed to disable their people. He risked his life to save many and the ship. Commander Hoffman is recommending him for a medal and promotion."

"That's good news," said Jake. "Mandy, you look like you've got a big secret you're dying to share. Come on girl, tell all."

"Well, okay. I've been promoted to Sub-Commander, and put in charge of my own department. I'm in charge of Social Engagement. The captain wants to re-open all the ship's facilities. He said that if we're going to live out our lives on the ship, we'll need lots of things to do."

"All of it?" asked Jake. "Even with the colonists from the planet we'll barely be over half the ship's human capacity."

"Yep, all of it. I'm not certain what the plan is, but I'm sure he'll tell me. We're scheduled to meet later today."

"And on that note," smiled Suvi-jean, "I'm due to meet with the senior staff in a few minutes."

"Will I see you later?" asked Amanda.

"You're coming with me, sweetheart. You're senior staff now."

"Oh lord, so I am."

Just then the announcement came over the ship-wide comm. "This is the captain speaking. All senior staff to the bridge." Suvi-jean took Amanda's hand and they left together.

On the bridge they were directed to the captain's briefing room. As soon as everyone arrived the captain spoke. "All right, people, we've survived the war, defeated the enemy, and now we have to decide what to do about them. Here's the situation as I see it.

"Humanity has been scattered, tossed out into the galaxy in small groups and left to survive on their own. We have no idea at all if any of the other colonies has managed to survive, and we have no way to find them. We do, however, know this one has managed to survive for over eighteen years, albeit in reduced numbers.

"Now, they attacked us, trying to steal this ship, why? Obviously, they wanted off this planet, wanted to go home to Earth. They didn't know Earth had been destroyed, and didn't believe me when I told them. They believed, and rightly so, that we'd never consider a trip back, so they tried to take the ship. They failed. Now we must decide what to do with them.

"Jeannie, I know you'd rather just leave them here. What are their chances for survival if we abandon them on the planet?"

She sat studying her hands. "You dropped off ten thousand colonists, Captain. Now, eighteen years later, less than seven hundred survive. Those can survive for a while in the caverns, but only with the help of the SUVI. They won't get it. Even if they did, the caverns are limited in how many can live there. Eventually an increasing population would cause internal stress, civil war, etc."

She sighed deeply then met his eyes. "No, they cannot survive."

"Suggestions?" he asked, smiling gently at her and knowing her response.

"Leave them, abandon this system as quickly as possible."

"I can't, Jeannie, and you know it. Please, help me here."

"Captain Baris, I will do everything in my power to help you. Tell me what you want to do, and I'll do what I can to make it happen."

"I want to bring those people up here to the ship and integrate them into our people. Jeannie, they're humans, and for all we know, together we could be all that remains of humanity. We can't leave them there if we can help them."

She nodded and let her shoulders slump. "Jeannie, what is it?"

"Captain, I, and the rest of the SUVI were enslaved by those people, subjected to cruelties, constant humiliation, and forced to do the work they couldn't or wouldn't do. If you bring them here there will be conflict unless you return me and the SUVI back to the surface and leave us there."

"No!" Amanda gripped Suvi-jean's arm tightly. "No, Jeannie."

"We could survive there, sweetheart, the others can't. This is the best way for the captain to ensure the safety of the ship and his crew."

The Captain was grinning, and he winked at Amanda. "All right, staff, Commander Sorenson has made a suggestion. Opinions?"

"No, definitely not." said First Officer Volkov. "Commander Sorenson is too valuable to the ship."

"Amanda's already checked in as against," grinned the captain. "Chief of Security?"

"Oh hell no. Sorry, Suvi-jean, but we're not parting with you."

"I'll second that," said the Chief Medical Officer.

"I vote no," said the Chief Engineer. "I still haven't had a chance to pick her brain yet." She grinned and winked at Suvi-jean.

"I completely agree," said the captain. "Jeannie, I appreciate the fact that you, in spite of your deep desire to remain on the ship, would offer up the swiftest and safest option. However, none of us are willing to part with you. What's your next best suggestion?"

"Sir, if you just bring them all up here you're setting us all up for years of conflict and disruption. You know this."

"Jeannie, what did I used to say when we played football in the corridors?"

"You said that if it was easy anybody could do it."

"The same applies here. Yes, I know it'll be a struggle for a while, but we'll manage, we'll learn, and grow together. Jeannie, we can't leave a single human behind, nor can we leave a single human hybrid either. Girl, we're all that's left of our species, we have to survive, and we have to help each other do it. Do you understand?"

Suvi-jean sighed deeply as she met his eyes. "You're going to make me practice again, aren't you?"

"Practice makes perfect," he grinned.

"All right, Captain, what do you want me to do?"

The captain gave a small sigh of relief, she was on board. If his long-range plan was going to work out, he needed her to embrace this idea fully. "We have to absorb all the colonists into the crew. First Officer Volkov will oversee that. I'll want you to help her find the best way to make use of the talents and desires of the SUVI.

"Above that, your job will remain the same, my eyes and ears on the ship. Keep a sharp eye out for any and all problems and help us head them off as best you can. Jeannie, we have to make this work, but we also have to look ahead to the future. We need to find a suitable planet eventually. Maybe you could put some thought into how we might hunt one of those up."

Suvi-jean smiled at last. "I have a few ideas," she grinned, "but first I'd like to spend some time with the Chief Engineer, get her input."

"I'm all yours, Jeannie," smiled Moira Duncan.

"Hold on," chuckled Olga Volkov, "before you lock her away in Engineering, I need Suvi-jean's help."

"Oh? How can I be of service?"

"The SUVI. They're still in the brig. We need to decide what to do with them, how we can integrate them into the crew, and how to make that work for them. I'd hoped that they'd listen to you as you were once one of their own."

"Yes, they trust me. I'll do all I can to help you, Commander."

"Thank you, Suvi-jean. Now, what do you suggest, start bringing up the grounders, work with the SUVI first, or ...?"

"We need to settle the SUVI first, otherwise there will be bloodshed as soon as the first grounder reaches the ship."

The First Officer rose to her feet. "Very well then, with your permission, Captain, we'll be about the task."

"Have at it, and good luck," said the captain. "Keep me informed as to your progress."

* * * * *

Commander Volkov led Suvi-jean back to her office where she picked up her side arm. "Okay, Jeannie, what do we do first?"

"First, we go talk to them, I explain who you are, and what's going to happen. We address any concerns they may have, then assign them quarters, close to my own if possible. You won't need that weapon."

"So you're nearby in case of trouble," as she replaced the side arm in the locked case.

"Yes, that."

"Are you expecting trouble?"

Suvi-jean sighed and headed for the door. "It's just a matter of time. Also, I'd like you to have one of the SUVI as your assistant."

"I thought you might consider that task."

"No, not really. I'll do my best for you if you ask it of me, but I think Nineteen will be better suited to the job."

Olga was grinning now. 'Any particular reason why?" She loved the way Jeannie's mind worked and knew she'd have sound reasons for the choice.

Suvi-jean started to speak, then noticed the small grin on the First Officer's lips. "Commander Volkov, are you teasing me?"

"Just a little. Jeannie, why Nineteen instead of you?"

"Several reasons. He has far better control over his temper that I do, he was the First Prime's enforcer, so he'll already be seen as an authority figure, and, as an older male, he was never chosen for sexual purposes, therefore he has far fewer resentments to deal with than I do."

Olga Volkov stopped walking and turned to Suvi-jean. "Jeannie, I'm sorry. I should have thought of that. You're right, and, as usual, your reasoning is impeccable. Nineteen it is."

They continued on to the brig which was full. Only the cells of the SUVI had open doors, but they were all still there. Suvi-jean stepped forward and called for their attention. "SUVI, come out of the cells."

They all silently obeyed. When they were gathered round she spoke again. "It's time for you all to choose your future positions."

"We choose?"

"Yes, Six, as much as possible. This woman is Commander Volkov, First Officer of the Reacher. She's in charge of personnel. Go ahead, Commander."

"People, it's my understanding you were all held slave on the planet below. Those days are past now, you're free to choose your own path in life. We'd like you to remain on the ship and become part of the crew. Unfortunately, we can't carry passengers, everyone must work for the good of all.

"We're the last of the human race, and as such, we need to stick together, help each other, and hopefully, survive and thrive. What say you, will you join the crew of the Reacher?"

"What other option is there?" asked one.

"We could return you to the planet," she replied, "but I hope you won't ask that of us."

"What will it mean if we join the crew?" asked another.

"As a crew member you will have a job, as we all do. Eight hours of work each day then sixteen hours of free time for meals, rest, and whatever else catches your interest."

"Will we have to obey orders?"

"Yes, if that order is issued by a superior officer. I understand how that would rankle you. Rest assured, this will be a lot different than what you're accustomed to. Before any job is assigned to you there will be several hours of instruction, so you'll know and understand what's expected."

There were no further questions, then one spoke up. "SUVI 5, we all trust you. What do you recommend?"

"I am no longer SUVI 5, I'm now Suvi-jean Sorenson. I hold the rank of Commander on this ship." She relaxed her shoulders and allowed her voice to soften. "I recommend you stay. I will admit, life here is not without its challenges. Learning to be completely human is a trial and a struggle, but all in all, life here is good. There are no pain collars, no predators, and it never rains."

There were chuckles all round at that. Finally, one man stepped forward. "First you set our minds free of the pain fog, and then you removed the collars. I will trust you in this, I will follow where you lead. I'll stay."

"As will I, for we should all stay together," said another voice as Nineteen stepped forward. One by one they all agreed to stay.

Olga Volkov smiled. "I'm delighted you've chosen to join us. Now, Nineteen, I'll need you as my personal assistant and advisor for the immediate future. Do you have a name you prefer?"

"I was Arron Steiner before I was infected, but that man is no more. I've been changed, augmented. I will remain Nineteen."

"Nineteen it is." She reached for her comm. "Commander Volkov to Ensign Borrows."

"Borrows here, ma'am."

"The SUVI have elected to remain on the ship. They'll be waiting for you at the brig, your contact with them is named Nineteen. I need you to assign them quarters as close to Commander Sorenson as possible, get them fresh uniforms, and then take them to the mess and feed them. Once everybody is settled in their quarters, bring Nineteen with you and join me in my office."

"Got it, Commander. On my way."

"Remain here, Nineteen, until he arrives. He'll take you to your quarters, get you fresh clothing, then take you to the mess where you'll be able to get a good meal. Ensign Borrows will also answer any question that may arise.

"Now Commander Sorenson, what should we do with the rest of the prisoners?"

"Blow them out the airlock." This brought chuckles from the SUVI and gasps of fear from the prisoners.

"You know I can't do that," chided the First Officer, a merry twinkle in her eye. "Try again."

"Transport them to the surface of the planet and leave them there."

"I could do that, but the captain wouldn't like it and you know it. Try again."

Suvi-jean grinned as she replied. "We could leave them there until Commander Hoffman gets around to dealing with them."

"Good idea, Suvi-jean. That's what we'll do." Just then a young ensign arrived. "Ah, Ensign Borrows, this man is Nineteen. He'll assist you to get these people set up. Report to my office when you're finished."

"Yes, Ma'am," he said as she and Suvi-jean walked away. "All right, Nineteen, did you not want to choose another name?"

"Nineteen is fine."

"So be it then," he said as he busily tapped away at the tablet in his hand. "Right this way folks." He led them out of the brig and down a long corridor to an elevator.

Chapter #10

To Catch a SUVI

More than a week passed, and Amanda rarely stopped. She worked, ate, slept, and worked some more. Suvi-jean felt the distance between them growing as Amanda became more of a workaholic, so she buried herself in Engineering. She and Chief Engineer Duncan spent considerable time on a secret project.

One fateful morning Suvi-jean realized she had to speak with Amanda, so she turned back from her path and sought out Amanda's new office. She arrived to witness a scene that tore the heart from her. She saw a man call Amanda *Lover*, pull her close, and kiss her. Suvi-jean fled.

* * * * *

Amanda was deep in a discussion with her staff of eight. They'd managed to get the five small restaurants, pubs, and the three theaters open and busy, but they were still struggling to get all the grounders involved in different activities with the regular crew. They were keeping to themselves, and it was her job to integrate them.

She suddenly heard a man call her name and turned to see him grinning at her. She knew that face, but it was a lot older. "Lathan?"

"It's me, Lover," he said as he swept her into his arms and kissed her.

"What the hell do ...?" Amanda pushed back out of his arms in time to see Suvi-jean turn and leave. "Jeannie!" She ran after Suvi-jean, calling her name, but the corridor outside her office was empty.

"Hey darling, that's no way to greet ..."

"Get the fuck away from me," snarled Amanda, reaching for her comm unit. "Security to the Social Engagement office, now."

"Manda, what ...?"

"Keep away from me, Lathan. You just put unwelcome hands on a superior officer."

"What? I just kissed you, girl. After all ..." Commander Hoffman and two other Security officers came in, weapons drawn.

Amanda pointed at the offender. "That man just assaulted me. I want him out of here, and I want him working someplace vile, that or shoved out an air lock."

"Look, I just ..."

He stopped talking as one Security man zapped him with a stunner, then rolled his fallen body over and applied wrist restraints while he was still twitching. "Keep your mouth shut or this will only get worse," growled the officer as he hauled the man to his feet and shoved him out the door.

"Ma'am, he called you lover and kissed you ..." said a young ensign.

"Yes, he did. Look, I was barely eight years old and he was thirteen when those colonists were set down on that planet. Lathan was my babysitter while my parents worked. The things he did to me weren't anything like what you might call love, but I was eight, what did I know of ... Fuck it, I swear I'll kill the bastard if he touches me again."

She reached for her comm again. "Sub-commander Drake to Commander Sorenson." Amanda was still running adrenalin and it was easy to read in her voice. The response she got shocked her out of her anger and broke her.

"I'm here, sweet Mandy. I will release you to your lover, but I'll mourn the loss of you to my last breath."

"Jeannie, wait, you ..." There was nothing but dead air.

Amanda tried and tried through the rest of the day, but Jeannie wouldn't respond. The ship's computer said her comm was turned off. Amanda hunted for her, but again, every time she arrived where the Computer said Suvi-jean was located, she'd moved on. Worse yet, no one else could find her either.

Three days of futile searching later Amanda went to the captain for help, but he'd been trying to find Suvi-jean as well, and having no better luck. "Amanda, what the hell happened?" She broke down as she told him everything. Once she'd regained her composure, he passed her another tissue and sighed. "What I don't understand is why in the hell can't we find her? We're on a ship, for Christ's sake, where could she go?"

"I have no idea at all," sighed Amanda. "I looked everywhere."

"All right, we've got something new on our hands here. We've got an alien of incredible skill on our ship and she's avoiding us. We know why, but we don't know how. Sub-commander, it's your job to find her and fix this."

"Sir?"

"Amanda, you're in love with the girl, that's easy to see. Her reaction to what happened is clear evidence that she fully returns your feelings. The problem here is, we're searching for a SUVI and we're getting nowhere.

"Let me see now," he mused as he inspected the screen on his desk, "I was looking over some of the attributes of the SUVI, each one of them is different, and I saw ... Ah, here we are. SUVI 13 has an uncanny ability to intuit the likely future. I'd say he's your best bet. Enlist his help and find Jeannie, fix the rift in your world, then bring her back here to me."

"Sir?"

"This stays between you and me."

"Captain?"

"Amanda, every one of the senior staff was once captain of his own ship, and none of us are getting younger. We've got maybe another ten good years left in us before we have to face reality and start considering retirement. That's why we've been so intent on finding a planet, a home. Amanda, there's only one person on this ship with the aptitude and drive to succeed me."

"Suvi-jean."

"Jeannie. The others all agree with me. Amanda, she's the only one who can take control and lead the SUVI as well as the humans. We need her, we all need her. Girl, if you truly don't love her then you have to bring her back and make peace with that, help her through the process, but if you love her half as much as I think you do, you need to get her back for reasons of your own as well.

"Leave your department in other hands for now, use whatever resources you need, but do what you need to do. Amanda, not a word to anyone about what I just said, not to Jeannie either. I think we should save that for a later date when she's feeling more secure."

"Yes, sir."

"Good hunting, Amanda."

Amanda rose and left the room with a soft, "Thank you, Captain."

She found SUVI 13 in the Maintenance Department. The supervisor called Thirteen to the office then left him with Amanda. Amanda looked at the man and swallowed hard. Thirteen was a hard-muscled man with a restlessness in him, and his disdain for her was clear. There was an edge to him as he spoke, and she stepped back from him. "What do you want?"

"I need your help."

He almost sneered as he replied. "I know."

Amanda's hands were shaking, and her voice trembled as she spoke. "Please. You know I'm trying to find Suvi-jean, please help me."

"Why should I? You proved unworthy of her trust."

That put Amanda's back up. She stopped shaking and got angry, taking a step toward him. "Listen you, I didn't betray her trust. That man grabbed and kissed me before I knew what was happening. I called Security, and as far as I know he's still in the brig. I didn't invite the embrace, I didn't want it, and if Jeannie had waited a moment longer she would have seen me fend him off. I need to find her and explain, to make her understand."

"You'll never find her, and so you shouldn't."

"Why, Thirteen? Why won't I be able to find her? Why shouldn't I find and explain to her? I have to find Suvi-jean, and I damn well plan to explain to her what happened, that it's her I love, and if she still wants to avoid me then I'll let her go, but not until I get to tell her first."

Thirteen didn't back down, but took an aggressive step toward her. "You'll never find her because you have no idea what you're looking for. You shouldn't because you're trying to change her, to make her less than what she is, less than what she can become. She's not human, she's SUVI, more than human, different from human.

"I can see two possible futures, one with you beside SUVI 5 and supporting her. The population is thriving, growing, the SUVI increasing in numbers alongside the humans. The other is you beside SUVI 5 controlling her emotions, keeping her unsure, afraid, and weak. The populations fail and pass from existence."

Tears came to Amanda's eyes, but she fought them back. She stepped closer and reached out to lightly grip his arm. "Teach me. Please, help me, teach me what I need to know to help her. Help me understand what she is, and what she'll need from me."

The man's eyes bored into hers for a long moment then he relented. "SUVI 5 is a hunter, the greatest of us. When first she arrived on this ship she would have memorized it, every nook, every cranny, tube, storeroom, everything and everywhere prey could hide, or she could escape to if need be.

"She's been hurt deeply, wounded, she'll be moving constantly from one place to another, watching for danger, eluding those searching for her.

"What she is. She is SUVI. We're the result of a mutation caused by a parasite. That parasite is endemic to a species that travels in large herds, migrates over long distances. The virus changed us so we could survive on that planet, made us somewhat like the creatures it came to us from.

"SUVI 5 is still on the ship, that tells me she's made a commitment to the ship, probably the captain, so now must remain on the ship to fulfil that, even though she'd prefer to leave."

"Leave? Why would she want to leave?"

"The needs of the herd rise above the desires of the individual. You're important to the ship, your continued happiness is of utmost importance to her, so to set you free to be happy she would leave the ship. Her prior commitment to the captain will hold her here, but she'll avoid you to let you be happy."

"But I'm not happy, dammit. I can't be happy without her, and I need to talk to her."

"Good luck with the hunt."

"Please, Thirteen, please help me find her."

"No."

Angrily she stepped back from him and turned away. "Why? Why won't you help me?"

"Because you need to prove your worth, your trust, and because you need to use your brain for a change."

"What? Listen you, ..."

"You listen. Think clearly about all the things I've said. Each thing has a message, a purpose."

She glared at him for a long moment then she got it. He was trying to teach her. The SUVI are aliens and she was still trying to deal with them as though they were human.

"All right, your brain works differently than mine. Your mind can focus completely on three or more tasks at a single time where I can fully manage only one. So, how does that information help me?"

"Once I get Jeannie back I'll need to keep that difference in mind at all times, I'll need to remember that she'll focus on the best way to bring the most benefit to the herd, even though it might be a bad idea for her. I'll also need to find a way to help her understand that the easiest and most efficient way isn't always the best. I saw this when the captain was trying to decide what to do with the grounders."

"Keep going."

"I'll have to find ways to help her reach her potential as a SUVI as well as a human."

He relaxed his stance only slightly, but she saw it. "So, how do I find a SUVI who doesn't want to be found."

"Use your brain," he replied, a slight grin starting to touch his lips. "Humans are lazy, they don't like to use their brains, they always want someone else to do it for them. You can do this Sub-Commander, and you need to. You need to do it for yourself, so you know within your own heart that you can be a worthy mate for SUVI 5, and to prove the same to her.

"I've given you all the information you need, now think like a SUVI and go find your mate." With that he turned and left the supervisor's office.

Amanda left and walked briskly back toward Suvi-jean's quarters. She hadn't been there in days. She sat down in their cuddling chair and thought. A long time later she rose and went to the mess where she found Jake and Carla sitting alone, gazing into each other's eyes.

"Hi, Mandy, any luck?"

"Hi, guys. Yes and no. No, I haven't found her, but I had a long talk with SUVI 13 and got quite an education."

"Oh?"

"Yeah. I learned that we have to stop trying to make Jeannie into a human, and start learning to accept her, love and enjoy her, as a SUVI. We have to help her learn how to interact with us, but still let her be what she is.

"I also learned that I'll never find her. She's avoiding me and we all know why. She's a hunter, I'll never be able to track her down, but you can."

"Us?"

"You, Jake. You owe Jeannie, and me. She's not avoiding you, just me."

"Me? So how the hell am I supposed to find her?"

"She's got a lot of pet projects going on in Engineering. One of them is that half-finished ship that she built. They brought it up from the surface and put it in the cargo hold near Engineering. I'm betting she hides out there, but sneaks away when I get close. So, here's the plan. You two get in a position where you can monitor the area without being seen. I'll go search the place. When she slips away, Jake, you hide in the ship. When she comes back you catch her."

"Catch her? How the hell do I catch her? Do you want me to use a stunner on her?"

"Only if you have to. Jake, talk to her, convince her to come back so I can explain things to her. Please, Jake, I need to talk to her. She'll listen to you."

"Jake," said Carla, lightly gripping his arm.

He patted the hand on his arm. "Yeah, I know. All right, Mandy, let's do this. Where will you be?"

"In Jeannie's quarters. I'll go straight there as soon as I leave the cargo hold."

* * * * *

Suvi-jean watched from her vantage point while Amanda searched her small ship. Tears leaked down her cheeks as she saw her sweetheart walk dejectedly away. She saw as Jake slipped into the hiding spot then she moved away as well. It was late the next day when she returned.

"It's about time you got back," said Jake as Suvi-jean stepped inside. She stood staring at him, and he wasn't sure if she was going to attack and kill him, or run away. "Come on, Jeannie," he said, patting the deck beside him. "Come sit with me."

"No."

"Why not?"

"Because you're trying to take me back."

"Yeah, about that. Now, just stop and think for a minute. You're a command officer on this ship, yet the captain's been looking for you for days now. Second, you're on a ship, we're bound to find you sooner or later. Thirdly, we miss you, all of us, Carla, me, Hal, and especially Mandy."

"No, she doesn't, she has her new lover now. She's just looking for me to humiliate me more. No thanks, I had enough of that when I was a slave. I ..."

"Oh bullshit, Jeannie, stop sulking and think. Do you really believe Mandy would do that to you?"

"I don't truly know, do I? I didn't think she'd ..."

"Now, stop right there for a minute. Go slow, think back, what did you see?"

"I saw my sweetheart kissing a grounder, a man I know and hate with a passion. I saw ..."

"Did you? Is that what you really saw? Think now, think about it. What did you see?"

"Jake ..."

"Tell me, Jeannie, what did you see? Exactly what did you see happen. Go slow, let it come back. You never forget anything."

"No I don't, and I know what I saw."

"You saw something, honey, but even though you remember all of it, it's still open to interpretation. Come on now, tell me exactly what you saw."

She stared at him for a moment before she replied. "I heard someone call her name as I stepped through the door. I recognized the voice. I saw him pull her tight and kiss her, calling her lover."

"Okay, now stop right there for a minute. Did she call him lover?"

"No."

"Did she step into his arms or did he grab her?"

"He grabbed her and kissed her."

"Did she kiss him?"

"Looked like it from where I stood."

"Yeah? So, did you watch or run away?"

"I ran away. Jake, what are you trying to tell me, what did I miss?"

Again he patted the deck beside him, and this time she came and sat with him. "Jeannie, what you didn't see was Mandy push him away, call Security, and have him thrown in the brig for assault. Girl, Mandy loves you to distraction, and she's tormented. You're hurting, Mandy's hurting, and I've been on this hard deck so long my ass is falling off. We need to get you home so you and Mandy can talk to each other."

"I jumped to a conclusion and ran away from her. She must hate me now."

Jake put his arm around her and gave her a gentle squeeze. "Honey, she'll just be thrilled to see you. She'll probably crack your ribs she'll hug you so hard. How about it, Suvi-jean my friend, let me walk you home? I'm Security now, don't make me arrest you."

That brought a soft chuckle from her. "That was a joke, right? You're teasing me, yes?"

"Yes, that was a tease," he replied as he gently hugged her shoulders again. "You're getting the hang of this teasing thing, no problem."

"Jake, seriously, is it safe for me to go back? Are you sure Mandy will really want to see me, that she'll be kind to me and not ..."

"She'll be thrilled, relieved, excited to see you, contrite for hurting you, even though it wasn't her fault, and more. Come on, Jeannie, you girls need to talk to each other. You need to fix this."

"You mean that, you're not teasing."

"Jeannie, I swear I'll never tease you in a mean way, not ever, not you ever. Okay? I mean what I say."

"All right, Jake. I'll trust you. Take me home, but you have to stay and protect me until I'm sure it's safe."

Jake smiled gently as he brushed the hair back from her wet eyes. This SUVI warrior, so dangerous and deadly, was serious. Inside that alien killer body was the little girl who'd caught a bad virus, and she was afraid. He lightly kissed her forehead and then rose to his feet, gently helping her up. "Let's go, little sis."

As they stepped out into the cargo hold he reached for his comm unit. "Security to Sub-Commander Drake."

"Drake here."

"It's Jake, we're on our way home."

"I'll be waiting." That voice sounded anxious.

Chapter #11

Mending Fences

Suvi-jean was nervous as they approached the door to her quarters. Jake was afraid she might bolt so he put his arm around her waist. "It'll be okay, I promise." She just swallowed hard and looked scared. He knocked, and the door slid open. Jake gently pushed her through and closed the door then walked away.

The two women stood gazing at each other for a long moment, then, with tears no longer restrained, Suvi-jean spoke in a halting shaky voice. "Mandy, why do I hurt so bad inside?"

In an instant she was held tightly in loving arms. "Oh my darling sweet Suvi-jean, my sweetheart, you've been hurt, and I've wanted so badly to hold you and make it go away. Come on over here and let me cuddle you."

She took Jeannie to their cuddling chair and pulled her close. Great wracking sobs escaped Suvi-jean and shook her body while Amanda cooed soothing sounds and held her tightly. Once the storm of emotion had eased she spoke. "Sweetheart, I know what you saw, and thought you saw. Now listen while I tell you what happened. Yes, I knew that man, and yes, he kissed me before I could fend him off.

"When I was a child he used to babysit me, we played games, as he called them. I was only eight years old, he was thirteen. What he did to me was wrong, and how he thought I felt about it was wrong, and whatever he imagined in his memories was wrong. I never liked any of it, ever."

"The things he did to me were wrong too. I didn't like them either. He always used the pain collar to make me scream when he ..."

"Shhh, hush now, sweetheart. I had him put in the brig and now he's got Jake's old job in Sanitation. He'll never bother us again. Honey, I'm so sorry to have hurt you so badly."

Suvi-jean sniffed and snuggled deeper into Amanda's embrace. "You're not mad at me for running away?"

"No, honey, of course not. You were hurt, more than I could have imagined. Jeannie, I searched for you for days. I was so afraid you'd never speak to me again, that's I lost you forever. Promise me that no matter what happens, you'll never run away from me again."

"I promise," came a soft child-like voice from her shoulder. "It wasn't just the man and the kiss."

"What? Jeannie? Sweetheart, what do you mean, it wasn't just the man and the kiss?"

"I came to your office that day to say good-bye," sniffed Suvi-jean.

"What? Jeannie, are you leaving me?" Amanda was crying now.

"I don't want to, Mandy. All I ever want is to be with you, but you're always so busy, you never spend time with me anymore, you're always working like my mother was. I just thought you didn't want to be bothered with me anymore like she didn't. I came to say good-bye and to set you free to concentrate on your work, and then I saw ..."

"No," sniffed Amanda as she squeezed Suvi-jean tighter, "no, no, no, not ever. You're right, I let that job take me over. Yes, I enjoy it, but I let it come between us, and that will never happen again, I swear it to you."

"Sweet Suvi-jean, I'm so sorry I wronged you so badly, and I swear I'll try harder in the future. You're right, I did neglect you, and you had no way of knowing what to do, no point of reference for what was happening. Please forgive me, sweet Jeannie. I'll do better, I promise."

"I thought you were getting tired of me. I thought you didn't want to be my sweetheart anymore. I didn't know what to do. Mandy, what should I have done?"

"Talk to me, Sweetheart. Just talk to me when I get like that. Please."

Suvi-jean snuggled deeper into her embrace. "I did try," came the soft voice.

"I know, and I didn't hear you. Never again, sweetheart, never again. Jeannie, I was so afraid I'd lost you, lost your trust, your love. Sweetheart, you mean the world to me, I love you, and I don't ever want another day without you in it."

"Mandy, what are you saying to me? Are you saying you want us to be sweethearts forever? Just us?"

"Yes, that's what I'm saying. I want us to be lovers, whatever that turns out to be for us, however that expresses itself between us, but I want us to make a solid commitment to each other right now. Jeannie, that's what I want, but if you're not ready for that, if you don't ..."

Suvi-jean laid a finger on Amanda's lips to quiet her. "I want that too, so much more than you can imagine, I want that too, Mandy. You know I don't want sex and probably not some other things like kissing, but I'll do my best to be a good companion for you. I won't ever run away from you again, I promise."

Amanda couldn't help herself, she fought the urge, but couldn't stop herself. She gently pulled Suvi-jean closer and kissed her softly. She felt the woman in her arms stiffen, but she held her gently and kept the kiss soft, sweet, and loving. Slowly Jeannie melted in her arms, and with a soft moan, began to tentatively return the kiss.

When their lips finally parted Suvi-jean's eyes were misted over again. "Mandy, why did you do that?"

"Didn't you like it?"

"You scared me, but yes, I liked it."

"Good, cause I'm going to do it again." She pulled Suvi-jean tightly to her and kissed her again, fighting to hold back the passion and keep it soft and safe for her lover. Again she heard that moan of pleasure and the woman in her arms returned the kiss somewhat more enthusiastically.

As their lips parted this time Amanda hugged her tightly. Suvi-jean enthusiastically returned the hug. "Mandy, why did you do that?"

"What? Kiss you?"

"Yes, that."

"Didn't you like it?"

"It frightened me at first, but, yes, I liked it."

"Good, because I want to do it more later. Right now there's something else I want to talk to you about."

"Can I stay snuggled down here on your shoulder while we do?"

"Yes you can, sweetheart, and I want you to."

"Good," replied Suvi-jean as she snuggled deeper into Amanda's arms. "What do you want to talk about?"

"About me being such a jerk and messing up life for you, for making you doubt yourself when you shouldn't, and for trying to make you human."

"Mandy, I want to be human again. I asked you to help me."

"Honey, remember when you first reached the ship on the back of that monster? Remember when you tore off the pain collar and swore to never be a slave again?"

"Yes."

"Jeannie, you were so strong and confident. You were a full SUVI then. Yes, a rebel, a woman escaping slavery, but you were a SUVI woman, a survivor, a warrior. You knew your own strengths, your power. By trying to make you over, I took that confidence away from you, and I'm so very sorry for that."

"Mandy, have you been talking to Thirteen?"

Amanda sat back to look into her eyes. "Yes, but how did you know?"

"I could hear his words in what you say, his passion, his conviction. Did you ask him to help find me?"

"Yes."

"And he told you to use your brain?"

Amanda laughed and hugged her tightly for a moment. "Yes, he did. You know him well, I take it?"

"Yes, I do. The opportunities were rare, but after I helped clear their minds, every chance we got he tried to teach me, to make me strong."

"Honey, how did you help them free their minds, free them from what?"

"Always a survivor had to fight the brain haze, to focus fully to understand instruction, even basic speech. The brain haze was actually the desires of the virus, the desire to escape, to join the migration, the herd. When I first discovered the berries, I brought some back and gave them to Nineteen, and then to the others. After that Thirteen was always trying to teach me to be strong. He always said everyone's survival depended on it."

"Yes, he told me the same thing. Honey, I believe he was right about some of this. Yes, you want to learn how to interact with humans in social situations, and I'll help all I can with that, but I need your help too."

"Of course, sweetheart, anything. What do you need?"

"I need you to teach me how to be a proper companion to a SUVI."

"I have no idea how to do that."

"Neither do I, lover, but we're going to work on it. From now on I want you to be my super SUVI, the woman who followed me to these quarters watching my ass."

"I'm so sorry, Mandy, but you're so devastatingly beautiful, I couldn't resist."

"Suvi-jean, are you teasing me?"

A soft giggle came from her shoulder. "Yes."

Amanda hugged her fiercely. "Oh gods, Jeannie, I'm so thrilled to have you back, and I want all of you back, my full SUVI, my warrior woman."

"Mandy, are you certain about this? She'll make mistakes, embarrass you, and more. People will fear her, her strength, her controlled power, they might organize and attack her, try to put a control collar on her again. You could get hurt and ..."

"And that's a risk I'll willingly take, sweet Jeannie. Honey, this ship is commanded by Captain Baris, your friend, not Farouk Bladon. He would never allow anyone to try to enslave you again. Honey, they may have been able to put the collar on a ten year old girl, but you're not ten anymore."

"Mandy, are you sure it's safe?"

"Was it safe for you to hunt those things with just knives? No, it wasn't, but you did it."

"You truly want me to be full SUVI?"

Amanda kissed her softly then pulled back to smile warmly at her. "Suvi-jean, I want you to be all you can be. Okay? I want you to relax and be yourself, I want you to stretch yourself, test yourself, become what you truly can be."

"Doesn't that scare you?"

"Honey, if there's one thing I'm sure of, it's that you'll never hurt me. It could prove exciting, perhaps a bit more uncomfortable than I'd like some days, but I'll adapt."

"Mandy, I want the same for you, but how can you do that if you don't give your job your full attention?"

"I can't with that job, that's true, so as of this moment, my main job, my primary focus, is you, to be a support to and a good companion for you. That other job just became secondary."

"Okay, if you're sure."

"Suvi-jean?"

"Yes?"

"Promise you won't withdraw at the first sign of ..."

"She won't, Mandy. If I let her loose, there's no going back."

"Sweetie, you talk like that woman you were is a different person."

"She is. Mandy, she's sleeping now, letting me catch up, experience all the things I need to experience to become a human adult. I woke her up to face the SUVI and First Prime, but put her back to sleep afterward. Was I wrong to do that?"

"There's no right or wrong to it, Jeannie. Honey, she's part of you, and you're part of her. I think you learned to suppress the Jeannie part of you so you could survive the slavery, and now you're suppressing the

SUVI part of you. Sweetie, I think you need to let her out and blend the two parts of you into one whole woman."

"If I do I'm afraid you won't like her."

"Suvi-jean, I love you, and I want to get to know and love all the parts of you. You're a complex woman, a human-SUVI hybrid, and you're my girl forever. Never doubt that. Just be yourself and let me love you. Okay?"

"Okay, I'll start in the morning. I want you to snuggle me like this for the rest of the day."

"It'll be my pleasure. Honey, it's all right if the warrior woman wants a snuggle too."

Chapter 12

SUVI Awakened

Amanda awakened alone in the bed. Startled, she sat up to see Suvi-jean sitting cross-legged on the floor, her eyes closed, and breathing deeply. "Good morning, are you meditating already?"

"Is that what it's called?" That voice was rich and full of confidence.

Amanda swallowed hard as Suvi-jean opened her eyes, they were a glowing amber. With a liquid grace she rose to her feet and favored Amanda with a bright smile. "Good morning, my exquisitely beautiful companion. I've done as you asked and released the huntress."

"The huntress?"

"I thought it would sound less scary than the warrior, my precious delight. My oath, you are so utterly perfect, can I keep you?"

Amanda laughed at Suvi-jean's teasing smile as those amber eyes returned to their natural green. "Yes you can, and so you must. Did you know your eyes turn amber when you meditate?"

"They do when I focus on the power of the SUVI, yes. I know we have a meeting with the captain, but is there time for food first, my treasure?"

"There is if we hurry. Get dressed and we'll go." Amanda swiftly washed her face and started to pull on her uniform. She felt the eyes on her and turned to see Suvi-jean watching her. "Hurry, get dressed," she admonished, blushing deeply. Grinning, Suvi-jean pulled on her uniform and stepped into her shoes, then held the door open for Amanda.

They walked to the mess hand in hand then gathered food and joined their friends at table. Jake watched them approach and nodded. "Hey there, warrior woman, where's my little sister?"

"She's right here, Jake, safe and sound as you promised," smiled Suvi-jean as she gently squeezed his arm. "She just invited me out to play."

"Okay, if you say so. Can I ask what's going on?"

"Mandy convinced me to stop trying to be human and be what I am, a SUVI woman. I'm thinking that perhaps I can integrate your little sister into the whole picture. What do you think?"

"I think you're scary as hell like this."

"Why, Jake? What is it about me that frightens you? You must know I'd never harm a friend, especially not you."

He looked thoughtful for a moment. "It must be a combination of things, Jeannie. You exude confidence, and danger. Is projecting that a SUVI talent, or is it just something you developed yourself?"

"I've never actually thought about it," she replied, "but you could be right. I'll see if I can pull it back a bit. So, did I see you coming out of Carla's quarters this morning?"

Carla turned to her, blushing furiously. "What? How could you ...? Woman, that's it for you. You're getting way too good at this teasing thing."

Suvi-jean leaned over and kissed Carla on the cheek. "You're adorable when you blush."

"Stop it, Jeannie. Mandy, make her behave. Hal, protect me."

"Whoa, leave me out of it, I'm still recouping."

Suvi-jean smiled and took a deep breath, her eyes had gone amber again. "You three have no idea how precious you are to me. Hal, you're a mad man, charging right into projectile fire? That was worthy of a SUVI, my friend, and I'm thrilled you managed to survive."

"Thanks," he grinned. "So am I." That made her laugh.

"Come on, Jeannie, we can't keep the captain waiting."

"Take me away, beautiful Amanda."

Amanda smiled and took Suvi-jean's hand. "Save some of that charm for when we get off work."

* * * * *

They arrived at the captain's briefing room to find the senior staff waiting with him. "Jeannie," smiled the captain, "I've got good news, we're ready to leave the system."

"I recommend we stay a bit longer captain," she replied as she took her seat.

Captain Baris leaned his elbows on the table and took a hard look at her. He nodded as though in approval. "All right, Commander Sorenson, you were the one in the all fired hurry to leave Elysium, why the change of heart?"

"Sir, at first I wanted to escape the range of the grounder's transports to thwart their invasion attempts. After we defeated that attack I wanted to leave to avoid bringing the grounders onto the ship. Now that they're here it makes more sense to stay a while."

"Why?"

"There are resources in the caverns we could use here, metals, machinery, food processors, etc. On the surface there are portable habitats still intact, crops in the ground, those things could be salvaged. Also, the personal computers of the First Prime and Second Prime should be confiscated and investigated."

"Jonah Thornton's on the ship, isn't he? What right do we have to confiscate his personal effects?"

"Captain, when I killed a garog, I didn't try to make a pet of its mate. Forgive me, sir, but you've brought more than one garog aboard the Reacher, and even now they'll be plotting. I'd like to know what form those plots might take as they manifest."

"I have to agree with Suvi-jean on that one, Captain," said the chief of Security.

The captain sighed and looked away, drumming his fingers on the table. "All right, whatever's left on that planet is fair game. If you can find anything there that would give you reason to proceed further, then do so, but if you can't ..." He left that hanging for a moment.

"Brandon, Jeannie, the planet is all yours, use whatever personnel and resources you need. Commander Sorenson, I see that grin of delight on your face, what are you up to?"

"Me? Captain, I ..." she laughed. "All right, I'll talk. Commander Duncan and I have finished that ship I was building; this seems like the perfect time to test it."

"That's right," agreed Moira Duncan. "I should go down to the surface and check things out for myself." That brought a chuckle from the captain. "I'll send my Second with Brandon to assess the possibilities of the caverns."

"Looks like I get the caverns, Jeannie," said the Security Chief. "Take a couple of my men with heavy weapons on your crew. God knows what you'll face on the surface."

"All right, people, get it done," said the captain. "Keep me informed. Jeannie, Amanda, a word before you go running off to play with Moira's new toy."

The others rose and left, leaving Suvi-jean and Amanda with Captain Baris. Once the door closed and they were alone he spoke again. "Jeannie, I sense something different about you. Are you all right?"

"I am, Captain."

"Perhaps I should explain," said Amanda. "Captain Baris, the past number of days have been my fault." Suvi-jean reached for her hand, but Amanda smiled and went on. "No, Jeannie, it's all on me. Sir, when Jeannie arrived both of you asked me to help her, and I tried, but I messed up badly."

"Oh?"

"Sir, Jeannie needed, needs, to learn to interact with other humans as an equal, not a slave. Without thinking it through, I tried to make her human again."

"And that was bad because?"

"She's not human, Captain, she's SUVI, part human, part something else entirely. When she arrived on the ship, she knew her own strengths, her power, and was supremely confident in that. In trying to make her over I unknowingly undermined her confidence, stripped away what she had become, and left her as that sick and frightened little girl who was suddenly put into a slave collar. I then threw myself into my new position and ignored her just as her mother had done, leaving her alone, unsure, and without guidance or support.

"I took your advice, Captain, and tried to enlist the help of SUVI 13 when I was desperate to find Jeannie. He refused to help me, but he did educate me, helped me to understand where I'd gone wrong, to understand what she truly is, and what I need to do for her. What I should have been doing from the start."

"And that is?"

"Helping her realize her potential as a SUVI, helping her to interact with humans without trying to become one of them by holding back a large piece of herself."

The captain nodded slowly. "What more can you tell me, Amanda? What else should I know about the SUVI?"

Amanda relaxed back in her chair and patted Suvi-jean's hand. "Sir, I believe these people will prove to be the greatest assets this ship has ever known. Sir, the SUVI part of them is herd oriented because of the virus being the guiding force of a herd animal."

"Okay, and this helps us how?"

"Sir, you've already seen it at work. Once a SUVI has accepted a new herd, they'll do all in their power to protect and serve the herd's greater good, even above their own best interest. Remember how Jeannie offered to leave the ship with the SUVI to prevent friction with the grounders."

"Yes, and other times too. Jeannie, is this why you suggested leaving before we could be attacked, and then again before we brought up the grounders?" She just nodded. "So that wasn't because you were afraid, you were trying to prevent undue stress on your chosen herd?"

"Yes."

"My god. What about self-preservation?"

"Don't worry, Captain," grinned Suvi-jean, "the SUVI will defend themselves with everything they've got, but unless directly threatened, the good of the many will always take priority."

"And that's what's different about you today, you've embraced that part of your nature again instead of trying to suppress it."

"Yes, Captain. Sweet Amanda convinced me to embrace all the parts of myself. This night past, while she slept, I explored and embraced that which I have become. I realize now that the woman Jeannie Sorenson might have been cannot exist. I've been changed, for good or ill, I'm SUVI now, so it's SUVI I will be."

"I'll be honest here, Jeannie, I agree with Amanda's assessment. It's good to see you with your confidence back. Go on now, go choose a crew for that ship before Moira leaves without you." He winked at Amanda as Suvi-jean took her hand and headed for the door.

As they headed for the docking bay Suvi-jean was busy on her comm. "SUVI 3 and SUVI 13 to the docking bay. Ensign Jake White and Crewman Hal White to the docking bay, come heavily armed. Sorenson to Dr. Reilly."

"Eamon here, Suvi-jean."

"Dr. Reilly, we're taking a small ship down to the surface, we could use a good medic."

"I'd love to, Jeannie, but I'm too busy. I'll send Carla."

"Perfect. Landing bay two."

"She's on her way."

"SUVI 5 to Thirteen."

"Here."

"We could use two or three strong men to dismantle those old habitats."

"Understood."

"What about me?" asked Amanda. "Got a job for me on that magic ship?"

"The ship is a bit too small to need a social director, but we do need a transport operator. Want the job?"

"You know I do, you tease."

Chapter #13

Explorer One

They arrived to find Moira Duncan and two of her engineers waiting impatiently. Several of the others were just arriving. Once everyone was there, Suvi-jean spoke. "People, this is Explorer One, a small ship of my personal design. Her job is to carry a small crew of explorers from planet to planet, or from system to system. Originally, I planned to carry the SUVI away in her, but that's no longer necessary.

"Now we have a new mandate, to explore likely planets as we search for a new home, a planet where both human and SUVI can survive and thrive. This will be her permanent crew, and today we have passengers, the Chief Engineer and her able assistants.

"So, if anybody here doesn't want this assignment, say so now and I'll seek a replacement." Nobody moved. "Excellent. Now, Three, can you pilot her?"

"I'll need a moment to play, but yes, easily," replied the gray-haired woman.

"Pilot you are. Thirteen and I will be the first off the ship to explore, followed by one Security man, heavily armed. Jake, Hal's still recouping so you're the explorer. Hal, this ship is armed as well. Commander Duncan can show you the weapons panel.

"Carla, you're our medic. This cabinet here should have everything you might need. Please take an inventory and let me know of any omissions you might notice. Amanda, this area back here is for transport, the control panel is here. With this projector here, you can transport objects from outside Explorer One up to the Reacher.

"Space survival suits are here in this cabinet, sleeping quarters and toilet facilities back here, and the weapons locker here will be stocked at a later date. All right, we're ready to go. Grab a seat and strap in, people." Suvi-jean noticed the puzzled look on Jake's face. "What is it, Jake?"

"Don't get me wrong, Jeannie, I think this will be a lot of fun, but I'm just wondering why we're using a ship when the transporters are faster."

"A transporter can land you at a single point with little or no protection. The ship can hover above the ground, explore for a safer landing spot, give you a safe haven to retreat to if needed, and more. This is a practice run, Jake. We'll get into the more serious stuff when we reach the next system to explore."

"Gotcha," he nodded.

Suvi-jean smiled and patted his shoulder then sat beside Amanda and strapped in. They could hear SUVI 3 in the pilot's chair. "SUVI 3 requesting launch clearance."

"Granted, SUVI 3, you are clear to launch," came a voice over the comms. The big outer doors began to open to a vista of outer space. When there was ample room, the ship rose and moved slowly out through those doors and into empty space. A moment later it banked and dropped below the bulk of the Reacher, dropping swiftly toward the surface of the planet.

The ship twisted and turned, did a few barrel rolls and more as it sped planetward. Suvi-jean called out to the pilot. "SUVI 3, if the Chief Engineer ejects her last meal onto my lap you will face repercussions." That announcement was greeted with laughter from the pilot's seat and a groan from the Chief Engineer.

"Just running a few tests, Commander," came the reply as the ship smoothed out. "All systems functioning within desired parameters." The merriment was clear in her voice.

As the ship leveled out above a rugged landscape, Moira Duncan unstrapped and moved to the co-pilot's seat. "Enjoyed that bit of payback did you, Number Three?"

"Sorry, Moira."

"The hell you are. Judy, I honestly didn't know you were on the ship. I knew you'd volunteered to join the colonists, but you weren't assigned to my ship. When we blended the ships, I learned you had been sent here."

"And then you learned how many of us perished, and didn't bother to check."

"I checked, Judy. You were listed as deceased."

"Deceased?"

Carla had overheard and came forward. "All the SUVI were listed as deceased," she said softly then withdrew.

"Moira ..."

"Forget it, Judy. I'm just thrilled to see you alive. What happened before was nearly twenty years ago. I say we let it go and be friends again, what do you think?"

"Seriously? You could be friends with a SUVI?"

"I already am, old friend, I already am."

"We're here, people," announced Suvi-jean. "Pilot, set her down. Jake, Thirteen, ready?"

"Ready," they replied in unison.

The ship lightly touched down by a number of broken and overgrown buildings. Suvi-jean released the hatch and stepped out into the foul-smelling air. Thirteen and Jake were close behind her. Suvi-jean looked all around then spoke. "I sense no danger. Thirteen?"

"Nor do I, Commander."

"Jake?"

"I got nothing scary."

"Then we're clear to explore. Let's go." They set out and swiftly moved through what once was a makeshift street. No danger presented itself, so Suvi-jean called out the engineers and the two men from maintenance.

It took a few hours for them to explore what was left of the original colony. SUVI 3 showed them where the colonists were buried in a mass grave. They didn't try to disturb that, but moved on.

The colony had been abandoned in a hurry and a surprising amount of equipment remained salvageable. Six more workers were transported down to help with the demolition and salvage operation.

The day was well along when Suvi-jean's head came up and she was sniffing the air. "Thirteen?"

"I smell them."

"Get our people inside the ship, quickly."

Thirteen sped to the task and Suvi-jean ran off in the direction from which she sensed the danger. Dammit, she'd been too distracted, they were close and moving fast. She turned and ran. Jake was waiting at the hatch when she arrived.

"Get in," he shouted, "get in." His weapon barked three times and a creature toppled to its side, kicking as its companions sped past it. Suvi-jean leaped through the hatch and Jake slammed it closed behind her. "Take her up."

The ship leaped into the air with several creatures clinging to her sides. "Hang on," shouted the pilot. A single barrel roll was enough to clear the creatures off the hull.

"Was anyone bitten?" asked Suvi-jean.

"No, no one was injured," replied Carla. "What were those things."

"Oraks," said Thirteen. "They're the creatures that carry the virus. Don't worry, it isn't airborne, it transfers by body fluid. You have to be bitten or have their blood splash on you to an open wound. We got away clean, Commander."

"Excellent," said Suvi-jean. "Three, put a visual of the landscape on the screen." The big screen slid easily down against the wall and lit up with a visual of the scene below. Thousands of the Oraks were streaming past the spot where the humans had been working. Behind them were packs of the dinosaur-like creatures that the SUVI called garogs. "So that's it," she mused.

"Apparently, we forgot the passage of time on the surface," said Thirteen.

"Yes we did," agreed Suvi-jean.

"Any chance one of you might enlighten the rest of us about what just happened?" asked Moira Duncan.

"Of course, Commander," replied Suvi-jean. "At certain times of the year, driven by the seasons, the oraks begin their migration. When that happens, the garogs gather into hunting packs to attack the herds of oraks. The original colony which we were exploring, was established directly in the path of a major migration route. What you just saw was what that colony encountered.

"When a migrating herd is driven on by the hunting packs, they will move fast. You've just seen how swiftly they appear and how aggressive they are, and the garogs that hunt them are worse. What you just saw was what wiped out the colony."

"Oh my god," said Amanda, "and those things carry the infection? You survived an attack like that and then the virus too?"

"Yes, we did," replied Thirteen.

"I was infected here," said Three, "all three of us, One, Two, and Four as well, but the rest were bitten in the relocation settlement."

"Relocation settlement?" asked Carla.

"Yes, after the disaster of the first attack the dead were buried in a mass grave, and then the settlement was moved over to the next valley. The next year that one was hit with similar results. By then we'd developed some medicines against the virus, so more people survived, but few indeed with their mind intact.

"The virus wants you to join the migration, be one with the herd. For most infected, that drive was too strong, and they died fighting the restraints, or they went so wild that Farouk killed them. For the good of the colony, he said.

"Shortly after that the caverns were discovered and we moved as much of the colony down there as we could, but many remained on the surface. Garogs and disease eventually finished them off."

Moira Duncan put her arm around Three's shoulders. "I'm so very sorry all that happened to you, Judy. I am."

Three patted the hand on her shoulder. "All done and gone, Moira. I survived and came out stronger. What's that saying of yours? That which doesn't kill you makes you stronger? In the case of the SUVI, that's quite true."

"Looks like they've all gone through, but we'll wait a while to be sure it's clear," said Suvi-jean. "Three, take her up so we can see more of the overall landscape."

"Aye, aye, Captain," grinned Three as she returned to the pilot's seat.

The ship moved upwards, and the broader landscape below appeared on the screen. "That's good, Three. Now, folks, see that broad valley, that's where we just were, and this valley here is where the colony was moved to.

"Up here is the beginning of the great plain where the oraks spend many months grazing on the vegetation there. As the season grows colder they migrate to the open plains farther in this direction. As you can see, both those valleys, so perfect for human habitation, are on direct migration routes.

"Only in the mountains, or the caverns beneath them, could humans be safe from the migrating oraks. That's Elysium, that's the world we were dropped on. Thirteen's right, we should've been aware of the season and known a migration could come through."

"On the bright side," smiled Amanda, "everyone responded instantly to the shouted warning and retreated quickly to the ship. We have a few more passengers than we started with, but we're all in one piece thanks to your keen senses and timely warning.

"So, should we go back to the Reacher and wait for a better time? Will there be more herds moving through?"

"There could be more," said Suvi-jean, "but I don't want to go home just yet. We have room enough and supplies for everyone here. I'd like to give you and the rest a unique experience, one you've never had before."

"Oh, what's that?"

"A sunset, beautiful Amanda, the one thing in this universe that could hope to rival your beauty. It'll still fall short, but it's worth the experience."

Amanda was blushing. "Jeannie, not when we're in uniform."

"Forgive me, pretty lady, whatever was I thinking?"

"I have no idea, but I'm thinking you're enjoying this teasing thing far too much."

Suvi-jean chuckled. "Three, how's it looking now?"

"It looks clear, Commander. The oraks are well past where we want to be, and the garogs with them, but if you want a sunset we'd better get down there."

"Land us on the ridge overlooking the original colony, Three."

"Landing. Hang on." The ship dropped swiftly then settled to a gentle landing atop a slight ridge, facing the fading sun.

Everyone stepped out of the ship to gaze at the sunset. Suvi-jean had been right, only Moira, Three, and Thirteen had actually seen a sunset before. They stood in amazement at the display of color on the scattered clouds. They almost held their breath as the sun sank beneath the horizon in a blaze of golds and reds. When it was finally gone, and darkness fallen, they stepped back inside the ship.

"Sleeping booths are back here, folks. They're small and spare, but functional. We'll spend the night here because I want you to see the other side of what you just experienced, a sunrise."

"First, we chow down," declared Carla as she started handing out meal packs.

Later, as they snuggled down together in the small cot, Amanda giggled. "Wow, this sure is cozy."

"Do you mind? Do you want a cabin of your own ...?"

"Not a chance, Silly Suvi-jean, I get to cuddle you close all night, and that's exactly what I want. Hush now and let me kiss you again."

Suvi-jean awakened everyone in plenty of time to watch the sunrise. They stood outside, gazing in awe as the sun rose red, then yellow-gold, and finally too bright to look at and they returned to the ship. One glance at the monitor and Jake spoke. "Incoming migration, Commander Sorenson, at least that's what it looks like."

She was at his side instantly. "Yes, that's another herd. Three, take us up. Let's see if site two is open." It was, and the ship settled gently to the ground. The explorers spread out, searching for intact habitats, storage containers, or anything else useful.

At one point, Suvi-jean noticed Three gazing at one structure. "What is it, Three?"

"This was Farouk's habitat before we moved into the caverns. Does it look like it's been recently used to you, Five?"

"Yes, it does. Jake, bring that weapon of yours over here."

He came running. "Jeannie?"

"Something's not right here. Watch my back." He nodded and followed her inside. The habitat proved empty of life, but it had obviously seen a lot of activity over the years. The solar power coupling had been jerked from the wall recently. Also, a cold storage unit stood open, the lock broken, but there was no sign of dust on it.

"I wonder what was kept in this," muttered Jake, his eyes still roaming about the room, looking for danger.

"I have no idea at all, big brother, but I'm not happy to find it. Send Thirteen in here, would you?"

"On it," he replied as he rested his weapon and stepped outside.

A moment later Thirteen entered. Suvi-jean showed him the container. "You're right, Five, this isn't good." He ran his hands lightly over the open lid and frowned. "Eighteen could tell you more."

"Go ask Amanda to bring her down, would you?" He nodded and trotted away. A few minutes later he reappeared leading another woman.

The woman looked at the container then her eyes turned amber and seemed to go out of focus. "This damage wasn't the work of animals, but that of humans in a hurry. I can't tell you yet what was stored here, but I can tell you it was dangerous."

"Any idea what happened to it? Who has it?"

"It was forced open, recently, by Second Prime. He was terrified of what it was, but he considered it so valuable he was willing to take the risk."

"Thank you, Eighteen. Do you know if Commander Hoffman is back on the ship yet?"

"Yes, he returned late yesterday. There are others working in the caverns, but he remained on the ship."

"I won't trust this to the comms. Go back to the ship, seek him out, and tell him what we found and what you suspect."

She nodded and turned away to the door. "Eighteen." She stopped and turned back to Suvi-jean with an arched eyebrow. "Thank you for coming, you're the best." Eighteen smiled as she acknowledged the compliment. She turned and left the building.

Suvi-jean returned to her search. She overturned every stick of furniture, opened everything that would open, then tested all the cracks in the floor. One yielded a small hand-held computer. It had been recently charged up. She put it in the pocket of her jacket and left the hut.

Returning to the ship she found Amanda and Carla helping to dismantle a storage shed. "Mandy, if I wanted to send up a souvenir to the ship, how close could you pinpoint the site?"

"I can put it right in your underwear drawer if you want," she grinned.

"Not only are you so incredibly beautiful, you're exceptionally talented as well. Is it any wonder why I'm so besotted with you?"

Amanda laughed with delight and took Suvi-jean's hand. "Come on, Commander, let's go put your souvenir in our quarters." They stepped into the ship and she went to the consol. "Commander Hoffman's office?"

Souvi-jean nodded then reached for her comms. "Sorenson to Commander Hoffman."

"Here, Jeannie, what's up?"

"I've got that orak fang for you. I'll transport it right onto your desk."

"I'll sit right here and wait for it," he replied. Jeannie laid the small computer on the transport pad and Amanda flicked on the beam. Hoffman's voice came on the comm immediately. "Got it, Jeannie. I'll put it right into the collection."

* * * * *

A short time later several Security men and women were transported down to the caverns with SUVI 9 to guide them. The search of Farouk Baldon's former offices and quarters was more than thorough. They also searched the former dwelling space of Jonah Thornton.

The search of the caverns also turned up several other things, things that sickened the Security people. They began to understand the cruel treatment the SUVI had endured, and they developed a new respect for them. Once the reports began to roll in, Commander Hoffman requested additional personnel. At least fifty of the grounders were suddenly under observation, eight of Farouk's former friends were confined to quarters.

Jonah Thornton was watched day and night, and he was getting nervous. However, as time passed, and nothing happened, he began to relax again. After all, he hadn't been confined to quarters like the rest. It escaped his notice that not one single grounder had been assigned to work with any of the ship's vital systems.

Chapter #14

Further Exploration

It took two weeks of full crews to finally get the salvage operation done, most of it from the caverns. The crew of Explorer One continued to search the two above ground sites until they were convinced there was nothing of value left. They were expecting to return to the Reacher, but Suvi-jean had other ideas.

They sat around, enjoying a meal of stewed roots and meat from an animal Thirteen had killed. Ever watchful for another herd migrating, they ate silently. Finally, Jake broached the subject. "So, are we going home now, or what?"

"I choose the *or what* option," replied Suvi-jean.

"Saw that coming," chuckled Amanda.

"People, we've tested the Explorer in space and an atmosphere, and we've tested ourselves as a crew. I'm well pleased with both."

"But?" asked Jake.

"Now it's time to do what Explorer was built for, and what she'll be required to do, what we'll be required to do. That is, if you want a permanent assignment to this crew. So, who's with me and who wants to go back to the Reacher?"

Moira Duncan chuckled at that. "Sorry, Jeannie, but I like my big engines. Why don't you explain more fully what you mean?"

"Of course. I am now, and always will be, committed to the Reacher and Captain Baris. The Explorer is simply an extension of the Reacher and will be used to explore likely planets for habitation. The rest of the time we'll be on the big ship as usual. The idea here is to be ready to man the Explorer when the need arises.

"I ask you all to consider this, as I believe it important for us to work well together, to become familiar with each other's style, methods, abilities, responses, etc. Planetary exploration can be a risky adventure, as we have already discovered. Working well together will increase our chances for survival."

"Makes sense to me. I'm in, little sister, I mean Commander Sorenson."

"I'll follow your lead," said Three.

"And I as well," agreed Thirteen.

"I'm in," said Hal.

"Me too," said Carla.

"At your side wherever you go, Commander," grinned Amanda.

In the end, the two engineers and the maintenance men also wanted to be part of the crew. Amanda transported the chief engineer back to the Reacher, then Three resumed her pilot's seat. "Where to, Commander?"

"Make a long sweep of the northern plain, swinging around to this point here at the edge of the mountain range." She pointed to a spot on the display panel. "Take your time; we'll do this as though we were scouting a completely unfamiliar planet."

The ship rose gracefully into the air, reoriented itself then moved away from the failed colony, heading north. "Jeannie honey, what's right here?" asked Amanda tapping her finger on the map.

"Mandy?"

"You want to end the swing right here at this point. Why right there, what's there?"

"Something that shouldn't be there, my insightful companion, something that shouldn't exist."

"Oh? What is it?"

"Another failed colony, but not a human one. The buildings are too small, and it's much older than our attempts to colonize this planet.'

The crew had gone silent. "I once found it while on a hunting trip. I was gone far longer than First Prime was happy about and I was punished when I returned, but I didn't tell him about it. There were many things I didn't tell him. At other times I explored it when I was supposed to be working on this ship."

"How did you manage that? Didn't he have a tracker on you?" asked Thirteen.

"He did, but I had a tool that confused that. When I engaged the tool, it appeared that I was where I was supposed to be."

"Ever resourceful, SUVI 5, I always admired that about you. So now we explore it again?"

"Yes, but this time with a full crew and proper instruments. We observe, record, measure, etc. and take it all back to the Reacher for others to study. Somewhere out there is, or was, another space faring species. I'd like to know as much as possible about them should we ever meet."

Thirteen winked at Amanda and relaxed back in his seat, smiling. "Perhaps, Commander Sorenson, you should formalize your crew a bit more."

"Thirteen?"

"You're the ranking officer, so you're in command. I suggest to you that each crew member would feel more secure, and thus better able to perform under stress, if they each knew their position."

Suvi-jean looked from one to the other of the crew and saw a number of shy smiles. "All right, my friends, Three is pilot, Sub-Commander Drake is transport officer, co-pilot, and my second in command. Ensign White is in charge of security, Ensign Marks is our medical officer.

"Now, we have two engineers with us. Ensign Billings, you're the ranking officer, so you're the chief engineer. That leaves us with eight maintenance men. Mr. Sacumbtu, as the most senior man, the maintenance crew is yours. Thirteen and I will be the First Explorers, that means that we'll be first off the ship if the occasion arises."

"Seriously?" said Thirteen, grinning. "Shouldn't the captain remain on the ship?"

"And I'm quite sure Captain Baris will do just that," replied Suvi-jean. "Meanwhile you can be the observer and watch the landscape below for anything of interest." Smiling, she stepped away from the observation screen and let him take the station.

Nothing of interest caught their attention until they arrived at the deserted buildings at the northern tip of the mountain range. They set about exploring, recording, and cataloguing their findings. The buildings were empty and had been for a long time. The only signs of activity were Suvi-jean's footprints in the dust of the lower rooms.

The rooms were so small they had difficulty standing upright in them, and the stairs we obviously built for creatures of a much smaller stature. There were places where technology had been attached to power supplied by solar panels which had been removed, but no tech was found. In the end all they found was a star map of the galaxy. They took it back to the Explorer to study it.

"What do you think, Three, can you figure it out?"

"I think I'd like to bring Moira in on this, Commander," she replied. "We've got the map, but I'm sure this module will have more information if we can just access it."

"Suvi-jean, what's going through that mind of yours?"

"Mandy?"

"Come on, talk to us."

"All right, whoever or whatever was here, they managed to avoid the disaster we suffered. There are no signs of graves, mass or otherwise, no bones of the dead. They obviously could breathe the same atmosphere as we do. I'm hoping that map, and any information on that module, will point us in the direction of more habitable planets.

"Obviously they gave this one a shot but passed on it in the end. Maybe they found others that were friendlier. Perhaps there might be one where they stayed, or one that would serve our needs better than this one."

"Oh my god, Jeannie, that's brilliant. We searched for ten years but couldn't find one. If these folks left a trail, we could get lucky. Captain Baris will be so excited to hear this."

"In that case, my delight, let's go report to the captain. Pilot, take us home."

"Aye, Commander, homeward bound it is."

The small ship leaped skyward, streaking toward the mother ship. When they landed, Suvi-jean spoke again. "All right, crew, you all have your stations. While we're on the Reacher, bring anything you think we might need aboard the Explorer. Make sure your station is as well-equipped and efficient as can be for our next voyage.

"Pilot, take that information module, and the engineers, to Engineering, see if you can crack it. Everybody else return to your regular stations. Mandy, you're with me. We'll report to the captain.

* * * * *

Captain Baris sat quietly listening to Suvi-jean give her report. When she finished he leaned his elbows on the table and nodded. "So we've got a possible traitor in our midst, a full cargo hold of extra parts and such, plus actual confirmation of alien intelligence. You've had a busy few weeks, Jeannie.

"You have my full support to enlist whatever personnel you need for the crew of your Explorer, for I have great hopes for that ship. The aliens aren't here, so that issue can be set aside for now. Right now, the big issue is what to do about Jonah Thornton.

"We have him under close observation, but our people haven't been able to discover anything from his former quarters, or his abandoned computer. What do you suggest?"

"Return him, and everything he brought on board, to the surface."

"Jeannie, you know I can't do that."

"Forgive me, Captain, but you know full well you can, and that's the safest course of action for the ship and crew."

The captain's back stiffened at that. Amanda reached for Suvi-jean's hand. "Easy, Jeannie, easy. Yes, it's the safest way, but the captain can't do that in all good conscience. To do so would make him no better than Farouk Bladon. Come on, girl, give us another option."

Suvi-jean's eyes had begun to glow amber, but she sighed and pulled back, allowing them to return to their natural green. "Of course, you're right, my exquisite beauty, the captain is far greater than Farouk could have ever been. Forgive me, Captain Baris, I meant no offence."

"You're absolutely right, Jeannie, I could do as you suggest, but I won't. Amanda is also right, we do strive to be better than Farouk Bladon. Give me other options, people."

"I don't know," sighed Commander Hoffman, "personally I like Jeannie's suggestion. All right, Captain, here's what we know. Jonah Thornton was Farouk's second, so he'd be privy to all sorts of things that we'd like to know. We also know he retrieved something from that habitat before they were brought up here, and we believe that something to be both valuable and dangerous, and we believe he must have brought it with him. However, we have no idea what that something might be, or where to find it."

"Have you questioned the prisoners, Farouk's confidants?"

"At length, sir. We learned nothing useful."

"And you have Thornton under surveillance?"

"Constant and unrelenting surveillance. Again, nothing. Either he has whatever he took in his quarters with him, or it's in storage and he's avoiding going near it because he knows we're watching."

"Suggestions?"

"Let me question him," said Suvi-jean.

The captain sighed. "As I understand it, you two have history, Jeannie. We've discovered evidence of what was done to the SUVI, especially you, and we have evidence that Jonah Thornton was a big part of that. I'm not sure having you question him would be in your best interests. Jeannie, I know you're offering me the safest and swiftest options here, but I have rules I must follow.

"Besides that, I don't want to cause you any more distress. From what I've learned I just want to find a way to help you put it all behind you, not bring it all back again."

"Thank you, Captain. In truth, the temptation to kill him might be too strong to resist. Perhaps Nineteen might be a better choice. Nineteen was Farouk's enforcer, and Jonah Thornton is terrified of him. Nineteen will have different issues, but he has much greater self-control."

"Jeannie, what is it?"

"I don't trust the grounders, Captain. Perhaps my personal experience clouds my judgement here, but I have a bad feeling about this. Can you at least confiscate his belongings and toss him in the brig where he can't get access to whatever it was he brought on board?"

"I wish I could, but the only hard evidence we have against the man is a clear record of what he did to you. The damn fool kept a diary. I'd love to shoot the bastard for that alone, but I can't. Now, sadly, all we have for current evidence is SUVI 18's intuition. People, it's a wonderful guideline, but we need hard evidence before we can do anything more than we're doing."

"Then let Nineteen and Commander Hoffman interrogate him. Believe me, his fear of Nineteen will make him sweat," said Suvi-jean.

"Captain," said the Security Chief, "why not let me handle this. By the book, I promise, but let me handle it."

"All right, Brandon, what do you plan to do?"

"Take Jeannie's advice, borrow Nineteen for a while, interview Mr. Thornton as well as the others we have in the brig. If that turns up any hard evidence, then I'll proceed accordingly."

"All right, Brandon, this one's your baby. Now, Jeannie, tell me how you first found the alien encampment."

"I was sent out to work on the ship with orders not to return until I'd made significant progress. It was too good to pass up. I set the machine to mimic the signal of my tracker, then went exploring."

"Your tracker?"

"Yes, a tracking device embedded in my neck, all the SUVI have them. I cut mine out and smashed it the day I came on board the Reacher."

The captain nodded. "All right, so you went exploring, and you found the encampment?"

"Yes. I was hiding from the oraks in that area and stumbled on it. There was no sign that anyone else had ever been there since it was abandoned. I explored it as best I could but had to return to work on the ship. I took the engine out."

"You took the engine out?"

"I didn't want it finished because he'd have taken it from me. I didn't dare let him escape back to Earth with that virus still active in him."

"Well, I guess there's only one thing left for us to discuss," said the captain.

"Sir?"

"When are you going to take me down to see that alien encampment?"

"Sir?"

"Jeannie Sorenson, if you think you're getting me to leave this system without seeing firsthand the evidence of alien intelligence, you're badly mistaken."

He was grinning, and she chuckled at that. "Sub-Commander Drake, please assemble the crew of Explorer One and prepare for departure."

"Yes, ma'am," smiled Amanda as she rose to her feet. "With your permission, Captain." He nodded so she left the room. They could hear her on the comms as she walked away.

Brandon Hoffman rose to his feet also. "Well, that's my cue. I have an interview to conduct. You go play, Captain, and I'll get back to work." The captain nodded, and Brandon left.

"Jeannie," said the captain.

"Sir, I apologize for my tone earlier, I ..."

"No, Jeannie, it's fine, I'm not angry with you. However, we have to find a way to temper your natural solutions with some basic boundaries. All too often the easiest solution leads us down a path that takes us to a place we don't want to be.

"Farouk Bladon was a good example of this. He knew what he wanted and look what that made him, what society became under his rule. We need fair and equitable rules of conduct wherein any member of society can feel they will be fairly treated, no matter what happens. Do you understand what I'm saying?"

"Yes."

"But?"

"My job is to present you with the most effective solution to a problem, is it not? It's then up to you to act on it, or not, as you judge appropriate, yes?"

The captain looked puzzled for a moment. "Yes, you're quite right about this. Let me get this straight, you understood this all along?"

"Yes."

"And yet you made a suggestion that you knew I couldn't use."

"Yes."

"Why?"

"Because that's my job."

"All right, then why the hell did you ..., dammit, of course, you're SUVI. I said I couldn't do it and you corrected that because you knew I could but wouldn't. Your intention wasn't to offend me."

"Of course not, Captain. You're my mentor, my friend, my greatest support, and a father figure to me. Sir, I would never deliberately offend you. Is that what my statement was interpreted as? Is that why Amanda ever so gently chastised me?"

"Yes."

"Hmm, I still have much to learn."

He chuckled at that. "We all do, Jeannie. Now, I just want to be sure about something, to be certain that you fully understand about the way our society is organized and how it's supposed to work. Tell me truthfully, if you were the captain, what would you do about Jonah Thornton?"

She gazed at him for a moment before she replied. "I'd question him with a grounder, a SUVI, and Commander Hoffman as witness. If I then still suspected him I'd put him in the brig until his quarters and stored belongings could be searched. If no evidence of wrongdoing was found, I'd apologize then let him go."

"And if you found something?"

"Depending on the severity of the possible damage to the ship and crew, he would be punished. A clear threat to the ship and crew would land him and any co-conspirators back in the caverns. I would not risk the ship and crew by keeping a saboteur on board."

"So, you think we should remain here until this is resolved?"

"I do, Captain. A few people could survive in the caverns, but if the ship is interstellar when the sentence is passed he will have to be kept in the brig for the rest of his life, using resources needed for the rest of the crew. There would always be the threat of him escaping or stirring up trouble."

"That's a bit cold, Jeannie, but I understand your reasoning. You do make a lot of sense. I just need to know that you can temper your natural SUVI impulses to accommodate we mere mortals, help keep us alive."

"Captain Baris, you must know my driving motivation is the survival and wellbeing of the whole group."

"I'm starting to get that through my head, Jeannie, I am. Come on, let's get to that ship of yours so you can show me the alien houses."

Smiling, she rose and led the way to the landing bay. They passed Nineteen on his way to the Security office. A knowing look passed between him and Suvi-jean. "What was that?" asked the captain.

"Sir?"

"That look between you and Nineteen? I saw you do that the day he killed Farouk Bladon. What is that about?"

"It's a look of agreement. We agreed long ago that we would hold the greater good as our purpose for certain actions, the greater good of the SUVI. Nineteen knew I'd already captured the SUVI, and he knew they'd be far better treated if Bladon was dead and you in command. He looked to me for acknowledgement before he struck."

"And this time?"

"He'll operate under Commander Hoffman's lead; no real harm will come to Mr. Thornton."

"No real harm?"

"Well, Nineteen might scare him a bit, make him sweat, but the real harm will be done by his own imagination."

"Jeannie Sorenson, you're a devious woman."

"Is that a bad thing?"

"Not in this case, no. Ah, there's your ship. Looks like the crew is all ready to go."

As the ship prepared to leave, Captain Baris smiled to himself. This crew was already a well-oiled machine.

"Sub-Commander?"

"Ship is prepped and ready for departure, Commander," grinned Amanda.

"Take us out, Pilot, destination is the alien encampment."

"Alien encampment, aye. Strap in." They sat and fastened the restraints as the ship rose easily and left the Reacher. Suvi-jean grinned as she realized Three was keeping the speed down and the ride smooth for the Captain. They soon landed, and she gave the captain a guided tour.

Chapter #15

Discovery

While Captain Baris was having a ride in the Explorer and a firsthand look at the deserted Alien encampment, Dr. Eamom Reilly was working in his lab. He sighed and sat back, shaking his head. He returned the samples he was working on and took out the back-up samples for the same two crew members.

A long while later Dr. Reilly sighed again and accepted what his eyes were telling him. There could be no doubt. These two people were closely related, perhaps father and daughter, or grandfather and granddaughter. "I wonder if the captain knows," he mused as he carefully returned the results to the restricted files. "I wonder if she knows."

Annoyed now, and wishing he'd never made the discovery, he began pacing about the lab. Finally he gave that up and sought out Olga Volkov in her office. "Eamon, come in, sit down. Tell me what eating at you."

"I have a massive ethical problem, Olga. I need your advice."

"Okay, shoot."

"I've discovered a close relationship between two crewmembers. One officer and one SUVI. The thing is, I doubt either of them is aware of it."

"How did you learn of it?"

"I was cataloguing the DNA of the SUVI and the computer announced a match."

"How closely related?"

"Too close. Normally, that wouldn't make a difference, but one of them is SUVI."

"Okay, I get the possibilities. You're trying to decide if you should tell them or not, or if either of them already knows."

"Yeah, that sums it up nicely."

"Ordinarily this wouldn't be such a big issue, so I can only assume one of these people is highly placed. The captain is Sivi-jean's grandfather, isn't he?"

"Well, shit, Olga, am I that damned easy to read?"

"It's what I do, Eamon, it's what I do. Now, as to whether either of them knows, your guess is as good as mine."

"So, what do I do?"

"Eamon, I can't make that decision for you, you know that."

"The hell you can't. As the ship's Chief Medical Officer, I've brought an issue of concern to the First Officer. Now quit stalling and tell me what I should do."

Olga Volkov pulled a decorative bottle from the bottom drawer of her desk. She reached for two glasses and poured each a portion of the clear liquid. "Have a drink of this, Eamon, that's what you should do."

"Dear gods, woman, is that actual vodka?"

"It is, and I claim doctor patient privilege. Not a single word to anyone about this or I'll blab about the whiskey in your office."

"Mum's the word," he replied as he tossed down the fiery liquid. "So, what do I do here, Olga?"

"You have to tell the captain, Eamon, you know that."

"Yeah, I guess. Shit, this'll throw a spanner in the works. Can't I just bury it deep and forget about it?"

"Too late for that now. You brought it to me, and now it has to come out. Besides, you know he deserves to know. So does she."

"Yeah."

"Yeah, what?"

"Yeah, I'll tell him."

"When?"

"Now I guess."

"He's gone down to look at the alien ruins with Jeannie and her crew. When he gets back I'll say you were looking for him and send him to your office."

"All right, Olga. I'll go back and work on my delivery," he said as he rose and stepped to the door.

"Eamon."

"Yes?"

"Save the whiskey for after you tell him, we both might need it."

"Yeah, because you know what he'll do."

"I do, and that's the last thing we need right now." He nodded then stepped through the door and returned to his office in the medical bay. Despite the First Officer's caution, he took a drink of the whiskey. Two hours later Captain Baris arrived.

"You wanted to see me, Eamon? Something wrong with my last physical?"

"Sit down, Captain. No, there's nothing wrong with your physical, you're still fit as a fiddle."

"Oh?" said the captain as he lowered himself into a chair facing the desk. "Then what?"

"Sir, I've been going through the medical records of the SUVI, retesting the DNA to be thorough and to be sure in my mind that all is well."

"Eamon, please get to the point before I reach retirement age."

"I found a DNA match, close blood kin."

"Me and Jeannie Sorenson," breathed the captain as he sank deeper into the chair. "You're certain?"

"I double checked. There's no mistake, you're either her father or her grandfather."

"Grandfather. My eldest son and her mother were lovers, but they split because she volunteered for the colonization. He was angry and refused to go with her. She was upset and avoided me the whole trip to Elysium. I always suspected, but she denied it, said she'd had a one-night stand before we launched. She wouldn't let me near the child.

"I asked the medical officer of the time, but she refused to confirm or deny anything claiming Helena had patient/doctor privilege. I had no grounds to refuse her passage to the surface. She knew damn well I'd never let her take the child from the ship if I'd known.

"Ah well, it's past time I retired anyway."

"Captain, please, you can't retire, not now."

"I have no choice and you know it, Eamon."

"She won't do it, Captain."

"Who? Olga or Jeannie?"

"Either of them."

"We'll see, but first you come with me while I tell Jeannie. She'll want confirmation." With a deep breath to brace himself, Eamon Reilly rose to follow the captain back to his briefing room.

* * * * *

Suvi-jean and Amanda were headed for the mess when they heard the announcement. "Commander Sorenson to the Captain's briefing room."

"On my way, Captain," she replied over her comm unit. "You go on, Mandy my darling, I'll go see what's up."

"Want me to come with you?"

"No, you go on, make sure Jake leaves some food for me," she grinned as she turned her steps toward the bridge.

She arrived to find the captain and Dr. Reilly waiting with sober faces. "Captain, Dr. Reilly, is everything okay?"

"Jeannie, sit down. Eamon has something to tell you."

"Doctor?"

"Suvi-jean, we recently brought up the medical records from the colony. I was going through the DNA of the SUVI and ..."

"Yes?"

"I discovered a close personal relationship between you and ..."

"The captain, yes, I know. Captain Baris is my grandfather."

"You know? How could you know?"

She chuckled at that. "Full genetic memory, Doctor, remember? I suddenly found myself in command of a ship, my own crew, and apparently the SUVI as well. I meditated, searching through my ancestry for someone who'd been an able leader to be a guide, a mentor, and Captain Baris appeared in my vision. I saw him as a young man playing dance with the ball in a group, I saw him with a child in his arms, and then I saw that child as a man in my mother's arms.

"I was thrilled to find that my mentor was also my grandfather. Not only can I avail myself of his guidance in life, I have his genetics to help me. It gave me full confidence that I will succeed as a leader.

"Why does this disturb you so?"

"Suvi-jean, it means that I must now resign as Captain. Once word gets out people will say I promoted you so quickly because you're my granddaughter; that I promoted Amanda because she's your lover. They'll say I deliberately didn't find a suitable planet because I wanted to come back for you. They'll say ..."

Suvi-jean reached over to pat his hand. "Stop, Grandfather, stop this now. Call the rest of the senior staff in."

"Jeannie?"

"Trust me, please, trust me now. Call them in."

Puzzled, he nonetheless reached for his comm. "All senior staff to the bridge, repeat, all senior staff to the bridge."

They sat in silence waiting for the others to arrive. Amanda gave Suvi-jean a quirked eyebrow, but Suvi-jean shook her head slightly. Amanda sat and reached for her hand. Once everyone was seated the Captain flicked a switch on his chair. "Listen up, people, what transpires here is to remain in complete confidence. I'll have your binding oath on it now." Each nodded their agreement.

"All right, we have a crisis on our hands. The good doctor has just discovered and confirmed my greatest hope. Jeannie Sorenson is my granddaughter."

He gave them a moment to absorb that then went on. "With this information before us, I now resign my position as captain and appoint Olga Volkov in my place. Captain Volkov, I respectfully request you keep my relationship with Commander Sorenson in confidence.

"I'm sorry, Jeannie, but you might get demoted over this. I ..."

"Oh stop," interjected the First Officer. "First, I decline the position, but I will hold that relationship in total confidence. Frankly, I was captain of my own ship for over ten years. Don't want the job, I'm getting too old for the stress. I suggest we move forward on our previous plans for retirement."

"Second that," said Brandon Hoffman. "I think it's our best bet."

"I'm in," said Dr. Reilly.

"As am I," agreed Moira Duncan. "I've seen Suvi-jean in action, she'll make a fine captain."

"What??? Are you all crazy?"

"Jeannie," said the captain, "we hatched this plot before we knew who you are, your relationship to me. We're all getting on in years, and this ship needs an able leader who can also hold the respect of the SUVI. They've chosen you for their leader, and so have we. Congratulations, Captain Sorenson."

"Have all you people gone completely mad?"

"Jeannie, it has to be this way. We need someone who can lead the SUVI as well as the humans. You have ..."

"You've all gone crazy," she exclaimed. "Every damn one of you."

"Jeannie ..."

"Grandfather, stop this ..."

"Jeannie, you ..."

Suvi-jean rose to her feet, her eyes glowing amber. "Stop it, Grandfather. Stop it and listen to me, all of you. You know who I am, now remember what I am. I'm full SUVI, remember what that means."

"It means you'd be perfect for the job, dedicated to ..."

"No, Grandfather, if you do this the people will know something's amiss. There will be resentments, the grounders will fan the flames, you could easily face a full mutiny, fights to the death, the ship could be torn apart, and these, the last humans, destroyed by their own hand. Think this through."

"Jeannie ..."

"No, Grandfather. You have to put aside your personal code of ethics here for the greater good. This is far too soon, the people aren't ready, not yet. If humanity is to survive, this information must remain a secret. You want me to lead you? All right, I will, but from within these walls. Beyond these walls all will be as before, and we will all carry this secret to our graves."

"She's right," said Amanda. "It'll be another five years or more before you dare retire to let Jeannie take the helm."

"Aye, that's the truth of it," agreed Moira Duncan. "It makes the most sense."

"Agreed," said Eamon Reilly and Brandon Hoffman.

"All right, Captain Sorenson," said Olga Volkov, "what's our next move?"

"Are we fully agreed that Captain Baris remains at the helm?"

"We are, Jeannie," she replied.

"Grandfather?"

"Jeannie, I truly wanted to acknowledge you, to ..."

"I know," she said, smiling as she gripped his hand tightly. "Only within this room can that be. Outside these walls we remain who we were for the greater good, for the survival of the many."

"All right, Jeannie, for the greater good."

She beamed him her brightest smile. "Thank you, Grandfather. Now, the rest of you, I'll have your solemn oath to hold this secret sacred.

"Swear it." She thrust her closed fist out towards them.

Amanda made a fist and touched her knuckles to Jeannie's. "I swear it. Secret and sacred."

The others repeated her gesture, and as the last fist touched her Suvi-jean opened her hands and grasped the others. Holding all their hands, she spoke. "For the greater good."

"For the greater good," they repeated.

Suvi-jean sighed and let her eyes return to normal. Brandon Hoffman grinned as he spoke. "So, what's our next move, Captain Sorenson?"

"Ask Captain Baris."

"Jeannie ..."

"All right, Grandfather, here's what I'd like to do. I think we should stay here for a while yet, use cataloguing the salvage we acquired as a reason, but I'd really like to deal with the Jonah Thornton issue before leaving this area. Also, we have no direction to take as yet. I'd hoped we'd get a few hints from that alien tech. That too will give us an excuse to remain until we have things more fully settled on the ship."

"Works for me," agreed Brandon. "Captain Baris?"

"That was my idea as well. Objections?" There were none. "All right, I guess we're done here, unless Captain Sorenson has more for us?"

"Please don't call me that, people. That could prove our undoing if it slipped out unintentionally. No, I have nothing further, except I'd like to promote Crewman Hal White of Security. He took several wounds, displayed strong leadership, and actually was instrumental in our victory over the grounders."

"I'll take care of that first thing in the morning, Commander Sorenson," grinned Brandon Hoffman.

"Thank you, Commander Hoffman," she replied, matching his grin. "Grandfather, a word in private. Stay Mandy."

The others left then she turned to Captain Baris and hugged him. "No one else must ever know, but I'll know, and you'll know. Also, I'll need your guidance as I find my way through all this in the coming years."

"I'll always be here for you, Jeannie, you know that," he replied as he returned the hug. "We're all we have left, Derek is dead, and so is your mother. It's just us now."

"Yes, and it's up to us to protect the last of humanity, make certain it survives."

"For the greater good?" he grinned as he released her from his arms.

"For the greater good," she replied as she stepped back. Taking Amanda by the hand, she left the room and headed back toward the mess.

The place was nearly empty, but Jake, Carla, Hal, and another woman were there waiting. "Jake, say you left me something," said Jeannie.

"You might be lucky," he grinned.

She laughed as they went to the food cases, selected a meal, then returned. "Hi, I'm Amanda," said Amanda as she extended her hand to the newcomer.

"Lilly Peters," replied the woman as she shook Amanda's hand. "Commander Sorenson."

"Hello Lilly," replied Suvi-jean as she shook the offered hand.

"Go ahead, Lilly," said Hal. "Now's your big chance, make it good."

"Stop it, Hal."

"What's going on, Lilly?" asked Amanda.

"Okay, I'll fess up." She slapped Hal's arm then turned her attention to Suvi-jean. "Commander Sorenson, I want to be on your crew, the crew of the Explorer. I confess I wouldn't go out with Hal unless he introduced me to you, so I could make my pitch."

"A resourceful woman," grinned Suvi-jean, "I like that. I'll tell you; I've already got more crew than I need."

"Can't you squeeze in one more? I'm only small, I don't take up much room."

"Your size is irrelevant. What's important is what you can bring to the crew, what's your skill set, and how can that add to the possible success of a mission? What do you have that we need?"

The girl looked crushed. "You're serious."

"I am. Every member of the crew has a value to the overall success of each mission. So, what's your skill set?"

"I'm a botanist. I worked in the hydroponics production area, but I want to explore actual planets, look for ..."

"You're in. What's your rank?"

"Yes, but I ... I'm in? Oh, oh, rank, spaceman second class."

Suvi-jean nodded. "You're a fully trained botanist?"

"Yes indeed, I trained for eight years with the chef botanist."

"You're in. I'll see about a promotion for you. First thing tomorrow, Ensign Hal White can help you gather whatever equipment you'll need and store it on Explorer One."

"A promotion? Are you serious?"

"Yes. Why do you keep asking me that? Do I not appear serious to you?"

"Easy, Jeannie," grinned Jake. "She doesn't doubt you, just her good luck. It's just an expression."

"Oh, I see. Ensign Peters, please find a different expression before you confuse me utterly."

"Yes ma'am, I'll work on it, I promise. Commander Sorenson, I can't thank you enough for giving me this chance."

"We do need a botanist on the crew, it's a natural. I should have thought of that before. Thank you for bringing it to my attention."

"Jeannie, did I hear you say Ensign Hal White?"

"Yes, Hal, I did. Commander Hoffman will make it official in the morning. You've earned that and more."

"So, what's the final verdict, Jeannie? Did the captain enjoy his trip to the alien site?"

"Yes he did, Jake. I think that's the most excitement he's had since the grounder's invasion."

"Grounders, is that what you call us?"

"Yes, Lilly, that's what the ship's crew call the people from the caverns. Please don't be offended."

"I'm not, Commander. If you can look beyond the past to give me a chance, I can accept that easily."

"You're a grounder?" asked Hal. "You didn't tell me that."

"You didn't ask."

"It never occurred to me. This is a big ship and I just thought we'd never crossed paths before."

"Is it important to you?"

"No, I guess it isn't."

"Look, Hal, I get that there's resentment because of what the First Prime tried to do. I wasn't part of that, any of it. I worked in the hydroponics with my father. We were still there when they transported up, and still there when it was time for everybody else to come up."

Amanda leaned across the table to grip the girl's arm gently. "Lilly, Hal was badly wounded in that battle."

"But I wasn't there, I wasn't. Hal ..."

"Easy, Lilly, it's okay, I'm not blaming you. You'll just have to forgive me if I say something stupid or bitter."

"Can I use it as blackmail material?" she asked, a twinkle in her eye.

"Behave," he chuckled as he gently hugged her shoulders.

"So, what was the big fuss?"

"Jake?"

"You were called to the captain's office then the rest of the senior staff. What's up?"

Suvi-jean grinned at him as she leaned closer. "Remember that list of deep dark secrets I have?"

"That's on the list too?"

"Yep."

"Little sister, sometimes you're no fun at all."

"I've heard that before," she laughed as she rose to her feet. "Come, my bewitchingly beautiful companion. The day is spent, and so am I."

"Dang," grinned Amanda as she winked at the others and rose to take Suvi-jean's hand. Together they walked away.

"Something's up," mused Jake as they watched the lovers walk away.

"Second that," agreed Hal.

"She was terribly abused," said Lilly. "We never met, as there was no need for SUVI service to the hydroponics, but we heard tales."

"She's trying to let go of all that, Lilly," said Carla.

"Understood. I won't do anything to remind her, I swear it. After all, she's giving me a chance to prove myself. Right now, she's my hero."

"Just go easy with her."

"I swear it, Hal. So, you've earned your date, what will we do?"

"Breakfast, right here before we gather and stow your gear in the Explorer."

"Oh, I'll be here with bells on. Walk me back to quarters?"

"Love to."

"Behave, my father has the rooms next to mine."

"Dang." They got up and headed for the door.

Jake smiled as he offered Carla his hand. Together they headed to her quarters. "Jake, you're going to be watching Jeannie's back closely, aren't you?"

"Count on it. You felt something going on too, didn't you?"

"Yeah, Mandy's nervous about something, and Jeannie's all tightened up. She worked too hard keeping the focus on Lilly and off herself."

"Yeah, I caught that. So it's need to know, and we don't need to know, but I'll be watching anyway."

* * * * *

"What's wrong, sweet Mandy?" asked Suvi-jean as she crawled into bed beside Amanda.

"I'm sorry, Jeannie. It's just that I think I blew it. Damn that Jake, he doesn't miss a thing and he can't keep his trap shut. He knows we're hiding something from him. He'll try to work it out of me."

"No, he won't, my sweet precious girl. He'll behave."

"Are you sure?"

"I'm sure. Jake's a naturally suspicious character. He won't trust Lilly until she proves herself. Until then he'll help us keep the secret."

"Yeah, so what happens after that."

"We'll tell him if we have to."

"Jeannie, we can't, not ever."

"Relax, my dear heart. That secret will come out sooner or later. I'm hoping and working on making it as later as possible. In a few years from now it won't matter at all. Right now, all the bitterness and resentments are still fresh, like a raw wound. Once we manage to integrate the grounders with the crew none of that will matter anymore."

"But ..."

"Stop now, my exquisite beauty, my intoxicating companion. It's time for you to teach me more about the kissing thing."

"The kissing thing?"

"I think I need more practice, you know, so I'm sure I'm getting it ri ..." She got no further as Amanda closed her lips with a passionate kiss. Suvi-jean moaned with delight and avidly returned the embrace.

Chapter #16

A Hint From the Past

Two women sat staring at a small readout from the module on the bench. It had wires of several colors leading from it to a dozen different instruments. "Dammit, Judy, I thought we had it that time." Moira Duncan thumped her fist on the bench in frustration. The screen flickered.

"Shit, Moira, do that again."

"What?"

"We got a flicker when you thumped the bench. We've got something loose somewhere." An hour later there was a scream of victory from the engineering lab. "Yah ha ha ha. Yes. We've got it. Okay, now let's get this onto our own devices so we don't lose it again."

"Commander Sorenson, please come to Engineering."

"On my way."

A few minutes later Suvi-jean breezed through the door. "Somebody here sounded excited."

"We are, Jeannie," laughed Moira as she grabbed Suvi-jean and danced her around the workbench. "Look, we've done it. We've got the information from the alien module. You were right, Jeannie. Look, they left us a trail."

"That's the best news we've had in a long time. Have you shown it to Captain Baris yet?"

"No," sighed Moira. "I was so excited I forgot that, you know, I just wanted to ..."

"How about I tell him myself? Have you got it over to our computers, so we can share it with the senior staff?"

"Almost there, we just have to ..."

"It's done," declared SUVI 3. She turned and saw Moira's embarrassment and nodded at Suvi-jean. "So, that's the way of it. It's as it should be, Five. This is to be kept silent?"

"Please, until it's safe to let it out."

"That could take years. Silent it is, but the SUVI will work it out."

"I know."

"They'll keep the silence as well. For the greater good."

"For the greater good. Three, do you want to join us as we share this with the senior staff?"

"Actually, I'd prefer to return to Explorer and load it into the ship's computers."

"Then so be it. Shall we go, Commander Duncan?" As they left Engineering Suvi-jean was on the comms. "Sorenson to Captain Baris."

"Baris here."

"Commander Duncan and SUVI 3 have deciphered the alien star chart. We thought you'd like to see it."

"Indeed I would. I'll call the senior staff to the briefing room."

"On our way."

* * * * *

The 3-D visual of the star chart hung over the meeting table. "We came past this on our way here," said Olga Volkov, pointing to the nearest planet with an alien marker. "We came past the star on this side, but had no indication that planet could sustain life. In theory, it's too far out of the Goldilocks Zone."

Suvi-jean looked perplexed. "Goldilocks Zone?"

"The sweetheart zone, the area with the right distance from a star to support human life," smiled Amanda. "It's from an old children's bedtime story called Goldilocks and the three bears. I'll tell it to you tonight."

"Amanda, are you teasing me?"

"Yes."

Suvi-jean sighed and rolled her eyes bringing a chuckle from everybody. She smiled as she went on. "So, this planet, the nearest the aliens visited to where we are now, isn't a likely candidate for human habitation. Perhaps they can survive harsher climates than we can, or perhaps the planet wasn't always in its present orbit. No matter, this next one looks promising."

"Yes, it does," agreed Captain Baris. "Do you want to head straight for that one?"

Suvi-jean looked up at that to find everybody looking to her for a decision. She sighed and sank back into her chair. "You're really going to make me do this, aren't you?"

"Yes, we are," chuckled her grandfather, "so what's the verdict, Captain?"

"All right, here's what I'd like to do, but I want your feedback on the idea, all of you. What I'd like to do is head for this second one, the one in the Goldilocks Zone, but, as we near the first one I'd like to take the Explorer out to investigate, see if we can learn more about these ancient aliens."

"Oh yes," grinned Moira Duncan. "Any chance I could re-apply for that job on the explorer?"

Suvi-jean laughed at that. "Sorry, Moira, but the Explorer already has a chief engineer, however, we've always got room for a consultant. You're welcome aboard anytime."

"Could you use a botanist?" asked Dr. Reilly.

"We just signed one on, a grounder."

"Lilly Peters," said the Chief of Security.

"You know her, Commander Hoffman?"

"I'm aware of her, Jeannie. She's been trying to wheedle a meeting with you for days, asking everybody who'd listen to help her make it happen."

"Hal brought her to me because she promised to go on a date with him. He wasn't aware she's a grounder."

"Do you believe she's trustworthy?"

"Unknown at this time."

"I'm curious, Jeannie," said the captain, "if you're not sure you can trust her, why take her on, especially with Ensign White on the crew?

He took a lot of wounds in that battle, and I suspect he may harbor a few resentments against the grounders."

"You're right, Grandfather, I believe he does. However, you've said we have to integrate the grounders into the larger group, to find ways to get past old resentments, heal past wounds. I thought having a grounder on the crew would give us an opportunity to practice."

"For the greater good," mused the captain, "even though ever instinct you have says to do otherwise. Jeannie, I'm sorry to have brought this on you."

"It's all right," she smiled as she patted his hand, "we have a challenge before us, yes? Can we not rise to it for the greater good?"

"Yes, we can," smiled Amanda. "So, the Reacher heads for the second planet, but the Explorer makes a side trip to investigate the first planet?"

"That's my desire, but I want everybody's thoughts on it. With any luck we could find more tech there, learn more about those aliens. People, please speak freely with me in this room. If this is a bad idea I can hear that."

"Oh, I think it's a great idea," grinned Olga Volkov, "I just wish I could go with you. About that, shouldn't the captain remain on the Reacher, send someone else to command the explorer? Perhaps I should go."

She was grinning, and Suvi-jean laughed. "I'll leave grandfather on the Reacher. If I stay here and take command, people would talk. I know full well that in a few years that will become my fate, so I intend to do as much exploring as possible before that happens."

"Damn," grinned Captain Baris, "for a minute there I thought I might get to command the Explorer and go play. All right, Jeannie, we'll do it your way. Yes, we all think it's the right idea, the more we know about those aliens, the better. However, you're in command here, you decide what actions we take. If any of us think it's a bad idea, we'll speak up, don't worry, but until we do, then you must assume that we're secure in your decision. Do you understand?"

She nodded thoughtfully for a moment, her eyes turning a glowing amber, then spoke. "All right, let me try again." She rose and pointed to the second planet on the star chart. "When we're ready to depart, the Reacher will set course for this planet. As we near this area, I will lead an expedition to this planet aboard the Explorer, the Reacher will remain on course. The Explorer will rejoin the Reacher somewhere about here.

"That's the plan, people. Opinions? Objections? Suggestions? How was that, Grandfather, is that how I should have done it?"

"That's exactly how you should have done it, Jeannie," he said, beaming proudly at her as her eyes returned to their natural green. "Where did that come from?"

"A younger Captain Baris, commanding the Reacher as she left Earth orbit," grinned Suvi-jean. "Once again, I thank you for your guidance, Grandfather."

"All my pleasure," he grinned.

"Jeannie," said Dr. Reilly, "that genetic memory of yours is the envy of everyone in the room, especially me."

She smiled and returned to her seat. "It's as much a burden as a joy," she replied. "Not all my ancestors were as highly principled as Grandfather. The farther back I look the more savagery and brutality I can see. I have access to a wealth of brutal savagery, a level of evil destructiveness that would drive you to madness."

"Easy, Jeannie honey, easy," said Amanda. "The past was like that, and the further back you go the more you'll find. Let it be what it was, find the good, the useful, and bring them forward for the greater good."

Suvi-jean turned to smile at her lovingly. "For the greater good, my beloved. All right people, where do we stand in readiness?"

"All personnel are aboard, the ship's stores well stocked, and we're ready for departure at a moment's notice, Captain Sorenson," said Olga Volkov.

"Medical bay is secure and stocked, Captain."

"Engineering is ready and anxious to test those modifications we make to the engines, Captain," grinned Moira.

"Security has an issue, Captain."

"Jonah Thornton?"

"Yes. That remains unresolved. You've said you don't want to depart until that's been put to rest."

"You're absolutely right, we stay right here until we get that settled. Did you and Nineteen question him?"

"We tried."

"Explain."

"He was scared to death of Nineteen. Every time I asked a question he'd look at Nineteen then faint. Bloody hopeless, the little chickenshit."

Suvi-jean was grinning. "What do you think, Mandy, let Jake and Hal have a go at him?"

"It's worth a shot," she grinned.

"Jake and Hal, the White brothers?"

"Yes," replied Suvi-jean. "They're friends, but Jake can be an intrusive bugger if you let him. Why not put that to use? You could watch from monitors and feed them questions to ask."

"I'm game, we're getting nowhere so far, what have we got to lose? All right, Captain Sorenson, I'll put the terrible twosome on it."

"Good. The Reacher remains in orbit around Elysium until this issue has been resolved. Is there anything further?" There wasn't. "All right then, I'm back to being Commander Sorenson. Captain Baris, the ship is yours." He grinned and saluted her then the meeting broke up and they all returned to their posts.

Chapter #17

Treachery

"Ensigns Jake and Hal White to the Security office."

"What the hell?" muttered Jake as he put down his fork.

"Beats me," said Hal. "Better go see what's up."

"Suvi-jean, why are you grinning?" asked Jake. "What have you done now, little sister?"

"You boys have a special task," she replied. "Everybody else has failed at this, including the SUVI. You're our last shot at it. Go on now, Commander Hoffman will fill you in."

Still puzzled, they left the table. Lilly was gazing at Suvi-jean. "What is it, Lilly?"

"This has something to do with the grounders, doesn't it?"

"Yes, but why do you ask? What do you know that I should know?"

Lilly sighed and stared at her plate for a long moment. "I know what was done to you, Commander Sorenson, when you were a SUVI."

"I'm still SUVI, Lilly, but no longer slave."

"Right, okay, I get the difference." She looked up, tears in her eyes. "Nobody should ever go through what was done to you. There was a man whose quarters were close to ours. We sometimes heard ... Well, it was horrible, and I'm sorry, but not all grounders are like that."

"No, but some are. Lilly, what needs to happen now is, we all have to let that be in the past. The grounders will never again have such power over the SUVI, but Captain Baris has refused to punish any of them for those crimes against us. That will cause resentments, I know. I give you permission now to speak to me if you feel I'm being unfair to you because you're a grounder."

"Thank you, Commander. How do you see this all working out, in the long run? Will we ever become equals with the sky-riders?"

"Sky-riders? I've never heard that one before."

"Sorry, Commander. That one started when the Captain first refused to invite First Prime up to the ship. You were already here, so you wouldn't have heard it."

"I find this amusing, and yet disturbing. Yes, Lilly, I believe that in a few years we'll all be just humans, equal and the same. So, what aren't you telling me?"

"Commander?"

"There's something eating at you, what is it?"

"It's my father. He's friends with a man who's friends with Second Prime. They're being all chummy and secretive. This morning Father asked me to keep an eye on you. To learn what I can about the Explorer and report back to them. I said I wouldn't do it. He was really angry."

"I believe you. Lilly, they brought something aboard this ship, something dangerous. I need to know what that is, I need to find it, and I need to know how to neutralize it. What else can you tell me?"

"Nothing, I swear it. Ma'am, please, my father doesn't mean any harm, he's just frustrated that he's not allowed to work in the hydroponic gardens. That's been his whole life, and now he's been relegated to Stores. I know he's ..."

"Send him to me. I'll be in the Security Office."

"Ma'am, please ..."

"I won't hurt him, and I won't punish him, Lilly. I'm going there on other business, and I can steal Commander Hoffman's office for a private interview. You can stay with him if you want to. Go on now, find your father and bring him to me there."

The girl nodded then hurried away. "Jeannie?"

"We need to gain the trust of the grounders, Mandy, and we need to resolve the issue of Jonah Thornton. Commander Hoffman is working on that issue, we have to work on integrating the grounders with our crew."

"Then you should be using my office, not the Security office. You want to put them at ease, make them trust you, not scare them to death. That'll only make things worse."

"My beautiful Amanda, this is what you're training is all about, isn't it?"

She grinned and nodded. "Want me to tackle it?"

"Yes I do, sweet woman. I'm starting to think we can trust Lilly. See if you can get anything out of her father, and maybe see if you can move him over to Hydroponics, under supervision, if necessary, but offer him some hope."

"Leave it to me, Jeannie," she grinned. "I can handle this. I'll contact you instantly once I finish the interview. You go play with Commander Hoffman in Security." She rose and strode away, Suvi-jean watching her go until she was out of sight. She reached for her comm. "Commander Sorenson to Ensign Lilly Peters."

"Here ma'am. We're on our way."

"Change of plan, Ensign. You're to meet with Sub-Commander Drake in the Social Engagement Office."

"Understood, ma'am."

Lilly and her father arrived and were ushered into Amanda's private office. "Ma'am, this is my father, Damien Peters."

"Thank you, Lilly. Please have a seat, both of you. Now, Mr. Peters, I see by your records that you've been a botanist for twenty-seven years, the last eight as the chief botanist in the cavern colony. Quite an impressive record, actually."

"Then why the hell am I counting nuts and bolts all day?"

"Daddy, hush."

"No, Lilly, that's a fair question, and it deserves an answer," said Amanda. "Mr. Peters, when the colonists were brought aboard the Reacher, Jonah Thornton, or one of his close associates, brought something extremely dangerous with them. As yet we haven't discovered what that is, or where to find it. I assure you, not one single colonist will get anywhere near a vital system of this ship until after this issue has been resolved."

He didn't speak, but his face told her much. "Now, having said that, and against my better judgement, I've been ordered by Commander Sorenson to have you moved from Stores to Hydroponics. You'll be working under close supervision, and won't have access to any vital information or systems until you can demonstrate that you're trustworthy.

"Lilly, Commander Sorenson has accepted you onto the crew of the Explorer. She has a tendency to work hard for her crew, to have faith in them and to make their lives better, that's why we're here right now. Remember this and be worthy of that faith."

"Yes ma'am. Oh, Sub-Commander, I can't thank you enough for this. Daddy?"

"Lilly ..."

"Father, I've stuck my neck out for you, and put my own career in jeopardy to help you. You know those fools are doomed to failure. SUVI 5 beat them at the invasion, and she'll beat them now. It's a fool's game that could get us all killed. Father, we're the last humans alive, are you truly willing to risk us all, the future of humanity, for a man who would barely acknowledge you in the caverns?"

Amanda saw his shoulders slump and he looked away. "Mr. Peters, if you have information pertinent to the investigation, please share it now before it's too late."

"They've brought a container of the virus on board. The plan is to release it and steal the Explorer, return to Earth."

"Mr. Peters, there is no Earth anymore. I was young, but I remember when we returned. It had been razed to the ground by the wars, nothing lived, nothing grew, the atmosphere was toxic, the waters poisoned, and all for political power. Now we have that same poisoned mindset aboard this ship, and I assure you, Sir, the same could happen here if these people aren't reigned in. I need names."

He gave her four names and she contacted Suvi-jean at Security. She then contacted the supervisor of Hydroponics. "I have a new recruit for you, Gerry. His name is Damien Peters."

"I wondered when you'd get around to sending him to me. Took your time, didn't you?"

"There are extenuating circumstances. He's to be closely supervised for the time being."

"You're joking."

"Only temporary. I'll let you know the minute it's safe to let him loose."

"All right, Sub-Commander. I'll take Peters anyway I can get him. What about his daughter?"

"She's been assigned to the Explorer, but you can have her while it's on the Reacher."

"The gods are good to me. When can I have them?"

"I'll send them over right now. Sub-Commander Drake out." Smiling, Amanda prepared an authorization chip and passed it to Lilly. "Off you go, people. Good luck."

"Sub-Commander ..."

"Go on, Lilly. Take your father to work, he's got a new job."

* * * * *

Jake and Hal entered the Security office and tapped on Brandon Hoffman's door. "Enter."

"You wanted to see us, Sir?"

"Yes, Jake, I do. Have a seat, gentlemen. I'm about to ask you to do the impossible. As you both know, Jonah Thornton's brought something dangerous up to the ship."

"He has?"

"Jeannie didn't confide in you?"

"No."

"Well shit ... all right, here's where we stand. We know that he, or one of his trusted friends, brought something dangerous onto the ship, but we don't know what it is, or where to find it. Captain Baris won't authorize a thorough search unless we get some hard evidence.

"I tried questioning Thornton, but he's closed as a clam. I tried with Nineteen as back-up, but the little shit just fainted at the sight of

Nineteen. Commander Sorenson suggested I let you two have a go at him. You up for it?"

"Oh yeah," grinned Jake. "Let me at him."

"All right, go find him and haul him in for a grilling. I'll be watching on monitors, so, sadly, no rough stuff. Good luck."

They saluted and left the office. They found Jonah Thornton in the mess, sitting with a half dozen friends. The brothers, hard faced, marched up to their table. "Gentlemen, you will come with us, please," said Hal.

"We've done nothing wrong," said one of the men. "We're not going anywhere with you."

"You can walk like men, or your unconscious bodies will be transported to the brig, and we can conduct the interview there," said Jake, fingering his stunner. "Your choice... Time's up."

He started to aim the stunner, but another man stopped him. "Wait, wait just a minute. What's this all about?"

"That's what we'll be discussing," said Hal, "now, the office in comfort, or the brig, naked under harsh lights, choose now and make it snappy." Back in his office Brandon Hoffman was watching on monitors. He was grinning.

They marched the men into the Security area and put them in individual cells. "Hey, you can't put us in cells, we haven't done anything wrong," shouted one man. Jake looked at Hal and winked. Hal turned and unlocked the cell and brought the man out, escorting him into the interview room. "What do you want? Why am I here? The captain will hear of this."

"You're here, my friend," said Hal, "because you keep bad company. Now, we know that Mr. Thornton out there, has brought something aboard the ship that he shouldn't have. We believe he's forming a conspiracy to commit mutiny aboard this ship, and we believe you're a part of that conspiracy. Deny it if you can."

"I certainly will deny it," he replied vehemently. "I'm part of no such thing. What the hell would be the point? Right now this ship is the only place we humans can survive, why the hell would we attempt to destroy it?"

"Now, that's what I keep saying," said Jake. "However, ..."

He was interrupted by the comm. "Commander Sorenson to Ensign White."

"Which one?" replied Jake, a grin on his face.

"Either of you. Jake, Thornton has a container of the virus on board, but we don't know if he has it or one of his friends."

"Understood, Commander. White out."

The man being interrogated blanched. "My god, the damn fools. You have to find that, destroy it before they can set it loose." Trembling, he collapsed into a chair.

Jake passed him a container of water. "I get the impression you knew nothing about this."

"I didn't. I swear I didn't."

"I believe you. Now tell me, of those men out there in cells, which one is the most likely to be in the know?"

"Ronca Elba," he sighed. "Second cell as you go out. He and Jonah were always thick as thieves."

"All right," said Hal, "you can go."

"Seriously?"

"Seriously. I don't believe you had anything to do with this, so, you can go." The man hurried out and closed the door behind him.

Jake looked up at the camera. "Did you get that name, Commander Hoffman?"

"I did," was the response. "Ronca Elba."

"I'm going to let him go, but I'd suggest he not get far from the door."

"Count on it."

Jake nodded then went out and dragged the next man in. He pushed him into a chair. "I'm not saying anything to you people. I have rights. I didn't do anything."

"For a guy who isn't going to say anything, he sure does babble on," said Hal. Jake just chuckled. Neither he nor Hal asked the man anything, they just sat staring at him. He began to sweat, then to babble on about his rights. Finally, Jake stood and opened the door. "Okay, you can go."

"What?"

"You can go," said Hal. "Go on, get out."

Jake hustled him out and pushed him toward the door, then turned to Jonah Thornton with a wicked grin. Thornton backed to the end wall of his cell. A glance at his friend told him the man had been sweating profusely. He wouldn't meet Thornton's eyes.

"Come on you," said Jake as he grabbed Jonah by the collar and dragged him out of the cell. He pushed him toward the interrogation room then slammed the door behind him. He shoved Jonah into a chair. "All right, start talking."

"I have nothing to say to you."

"Moron, ..."

"Easy, Jake, easy," grinned Hal. "Mr. Thornton, let me tell you what we know, and then you can fill in the blanks, okay? We know you broke into the surface dwelling of the First Prime. We know you took something from there and brought it on board the Reacher. We also know that it's a container of the virus that killed so many of the colonists.

"Now, what I want to know is, what the fuck's wrong with your head? Do you seriously want to release that virus into this ship, to actually destroy the last humans in existence? I don't get it, I just don't. Where's the gain? What do you expect to get out of this? What's in it for you?"

Commander Hoffman sat forward as he noticed the sly smile on Thornton's face. "Revenge," said the small man. "You goddam fools, you destroyed everything. I had it all set up. I knew Farouk would fail, but I should have taken his place.

"Yes, me, I should have been First Prime, but no, you fucking morons had to take that slave collar off SUVI 5 and ruin everything. She's out of control now, free and on the loose. You have no idea what you've done, what she's capable of, what she'll do, or what she'll become, and you've lost all control of her. You're all as good as dead anyway."

"Jeannie? What the hell are you raving about?"

Thornton lunged ahead and grabbed Hal by the collar. "She was mine, mine. With Faruk dead she was mine." He released Hal and melted back into his chair, weeping. "Mine. She was mine. Nothing left to live for now, but I'll take all of you with me, every damn one of you.

"She'll probably survive though, she can survive anything, anything, ... mine, gone free, gone."

"Where is it?" asked Jake.

"Gone."

"Come on, Thornton, focus. Where is it?"

"Should have been mine. Gone."

"Shit," growled Jake, "he's lost it. Commander, did you get all that? Have we got cause for a search now?"

"We sure as hell do, and it's already under way. Throw that piece of misery back into a cell and come to my office."

They put Jonah Thornton back into a cell and entered Brandon's office to find him with three glasses on his desk and a bottle of something golden in his hand. "Either of you men ever tasted real whiskey before?"

"Once," said Jake, "tasted like shit and burned all the way down."

"It's better the second time around," grinned the Security Chief. He poured a small shot into each glass then passed them each one.

"Gentlemen, that was masterfully done. Congratulations. We'll use Jeannie's toast." He held up his glass. "For the greater good."

"For the greater good." They repeated the toast then drank, each one sucking in his breath and making a face.

"Jesus," said Brandon, "I've never understood how anybody could get addicted to this shit." Jake just chuckled; he didn't trust his voice.

* * * * *

The Senior Staff sat with Captain Baris and listened to the interview with Jonah Thornton. Jeannie sat stone faced while the recording played out. "Has the search turned up anything?" she asked as the recording finished. Her eyes were glowing amber, and they could all feel the tension in her.

"Not yet," replied Brandon Hoffman. "It's a work in progress."

"Have Jake and Hal interviewed the rest of those men?"

"Yes. They've got a few more names of people to question. The rats are deserting the sinking ship now, and they're falling over themselves to turn each other in."

"Jeannie?"

"Yes Grandfather?"

"What are you going to do?"

With a visible effort she regained control and sat beside Amanda. Amanda took her hand and gently squeezed; Suvi-jean's eyes returned to their natural green. "Nothing at this time. Commander Hoffman has things well in hand, Jonah Thornton is being kept in isolation, and the investigation is ongoing. I'm content to leave it in the hands of our Security people.

"The virus, those fools actually brought it on board the ship. Dr. Reilly, did you learn anything interesting from those berries?"

"I did, actually. I managed to isolate the active ingredient, and I've been working on an antivirus. I could use more berries."

"I'll see to it. So, they want the Explorer, do they? Well they can't have it. Amanda, my beloved, quietly gather the crew and take the ship down to the planet. Tell Thirteen he's the Security until Jake and Hal are finished here. Gather berries for Dr. Reilly, explore as you desire, but keep that ship out of the reach of the conspirators."

"Aren't you coming?"

"No love, I'm the captain, I must remain here until we finish this. I'll miss you terribly while you're gone."

"And I you, my sweet Suvi-jean. I'll let you know when I'm off the ship." She rose and quietly left the room.

"Now what?" asked Olga Volkov.

"Now we wait," said Suvi-jean. "I'll be in Security with Commander Hoffman if needed." With that the meeting broke up.

"We'll find it, Jeannie," said Brandon as they walked toward Security.

"I know," she replied softly, "I know."

Chapter #18

Closure

The rest of the day turned up nothing more useful and Suvi-jean retired to the mess for a meal before going to her rest. She found Jake and Hal sitting alone at table. Gathering up a plate of food, she joined them. "Hey Guys."

"Jeannie, my sister, where are the rest of our people?"

"The rest of our people, Jake?"

"Our girlfriends," chuckled Hal, "Carla and Lilly, Mandy for that matter."

"They're on the Explorer."

"Oh? You sent the Explorer out without telling us? Without going yourself?"

"There wasn't time, Jake," she replied, refusing to rise to his tone. "You and Hal were busy interviewing possible mutineers. I learned that they planned to destroy the Reacher, and steal the Explorer for their escape. I had Mandy take her out with orders to stay away from the Reacher until I sound the all-clear."

"That makes sense, but there's more, isn't there? I'm your Chief of Security on the Explorer. You need to trust me. How am I supposed to function if you don't keep me in the loop? You knew about Thornton long before we were called in, didn't you?"

Suvi-jean sat back, a hint of amber creeping into her eyes. "Are you chastising me, Ensign White?"

Jake didn't back down. "Yes I am, Jeannie, as your big brother, and as your Chief of Security. Jeannie, I need to know this shit if I'm going to protect you, help you do whatever it is you're trying to do. God only knows why, but you pulled me out of the crap, got me promoted, and more. Little sister, you trusted me when you were hurt and lost, I'm asking for that trust again."

Slowly the amber left her eyes and she relaxed. "Man, you're a nosy bugger, Jake."

"I'm a security guy, it's in my nature. Come on, sis, talk to us."

"All right, but you take this information to the grave unless I release you from it. Your oath on it now." Both men nodded. "Yes, I knew about it, but we were trying to keep it quiet and find whatever it was."

"Okay, fine," said Jake, "but what's really going on?"

"Two things. First, we have to find that virus and get it off the ship, and then deal with the conspirators."

"And the second thing?"

"Jake, any hint of this could start riots on the ship. This information must be kept silent, at least for the foreseeable future."

"We'll keep quiet, Jeannie. This has had you messed up for a while now. Talk to us, let us help."

"Captain Baris is my grandfather."

"What???"

"Hush."

Jake cleared his throat then leaned his elbows on the table. "Jesus, Jeannie. Does he know?"

"Yes, Dr. Reilly discovered this when he was cataloguing the medical records from the caverns."

"All right, tell me the rest of it."

"Damn, you're good."

"Quit stalling, talk to big brother," he grinned.

"The Senior Staff are all close to retirement age, all former captains. By common agreement among them, I've been promoted to captain of the Reacher."

Jake turned to Hal. "See, didn't I tell you? Pay up."

Hal sighed and slid the ring off his finger and passed it to Jake who put in on, grinning with delight. Seeing Suvi-jean's raised eyebrow, Hal spoke. "Great Grandfather's ring, I wear it until I lose a bet then Jake wears it until I win it back. He bet me that you've been in command for days."

"Longer," sighed Suvi-jean. "Look, guys, I really need you to find that damned virus."

"I can probably do it," said Jake, "but it's highly unethical."

"I'm not Grandfather, do what you have to, but find that virus."

"Okay, but I'll need you to help me set it up."

"Oh?"

"Yeah, here's what I have in mind." He told her and her eyes opened wide. "I was going to use Carla or Mandy, but you sent them away, so we need a new volunteer."

"Leave that with me, we'll set it up in the morning."

* * * * *

The next morning Suvi-jean was in the Security Office, chatting with Brandon when his second arrived. "Okay, Boss, what's so damn urgent that you had to call me in eight hours early?"

"Sheila Singh, I have an important assignment for you, one that you are uniquely qualified for. Jeannie?"

"Oh yes, Sub-Commander Singh is exceptionally beautiful. She's perfect."

With wide eyes, Sheila Singh started to back away. "All right, what the hell are you two up to, and I want it on record that I want no part of it."

Suvi-jean chuckled. "Don't run away yet, just listen. We need to find that virus, and every day that goes by without locating it endangers the ship and crew. Now, here's what we have planned ..."

When she finished Sheila's eyes were wide with shock and disbelief. "What??? Are you completely insane? You are, you're both mad as hatters. And you want me to ...? Thornton was right, she's crazy, and now you've gone crazy, we're all crazy ..."

"Does that mean you'll do it?" asked Suvi-jean, a grin playing at her lips.

Sheila gave her the *look*. "You want me to be the sexy girlfriend. You do realize I'm nearly sixty years old?"

"But you look so much younger," exclaimed Suvi-jean. "You're exceptionally beautiful, you move with the grace of a dancer, you have that confidence that a woman can only gain through experience, and ..."

"You get away from me, Suvi-jean Sorenson. My god, does Amanda know you talk like that?"

"She does," grinned Suvi-jean. "She likes it."

Sheila started laughing. "All right, you two, are you sure about this?"

"We can't find it, Sheila," sighed Brandon. "We need that devious little shit to show us where it is. If we let him out, he'll smell a rat. This way he'll believe he got lucky and outsmarted us."

"So tell me, is the security guard in on this? You don't want him to panic and run away at first sight of me."

"I'll bring him into the loop while you go change into something more ..."

"Don't say it, Suvi-jean, don't you dare even think it. God, you two are out of your minds, I'm out of my mind for listening to you, we're all going crazy ..." She was still muttering as she fled to her quarters to change from her uniform.

While Sheila Singh was turning herself into the girlfriend character, Suvi-jean entered the brig area. Jonah Thornton's eyes followed her every move as she approached the security guard at his station. "I need you to read and sign off on this," she said as she passed him a tablet.

Puzzled, he glanced down and began to read. His eyes suddenly opened wide and he looked up at her. She shook her head ever so slightly and he returned his gaze to the tablet. When he finished he looked up again and she nodded imperceptibly. He made a motion over the tablet then handed it back to her. "There you are, Commander, all set to go."

She thanked him and left the room, Thornton's eyes following her ever step. A few moments later another woman opened the door and entered. She was beautiful, wearing a tight sweater and a short skirt with high heeled shoes. She moved slowly toward the security man whose eyes were glued to her form.

"Hey there. So, this is where they hide you away all the time, leaving me all alone. I thought you might like some company to break up the monotony of the day."

"I must admit, you're a delightful distraction, pretty lady."

"There's no need to be so formal, lover," she purred as she slid into his arms. "We're all alone here." She turned him slightly, so his back was to Jonah Thornton's cell, and raised her lips for a kiss.

As the guard pulled her closer, he leaned back against the control panel. Jonah Thornton's eyes opened wide as he heard the lock on his cell door click open.

He looked up, but the guard and his woman were kissing, ignoring him completely. Hesitantly, he approached the door and slid it open. He glanced up again as the guard moaned with delight, lifted the woman off her feet, and kissed her deeply. She wrapped her legs around his waist as Jonah Thornton slipped out the door.

"All right, he's gone," she whispered as she released her grip on his waist and lowered her feet to the floor. "You can put me down now."

"Do I have to?" he grinned.

"Yes, you have to," she laughed as she slapped at his arm.

She headed for the door, but his voice stopped her. "Sub-Commander Singh?"

"Yes?" she asked as she stopped and turned to face him.

"That kiss awakened a part of me I thought long since dead. Any chances for a dinner date and a good-night kiss?"

She gave him a long look. He was younger, but there was a touch of gray at his temples, and that boyish grin, along with her lipstick on his face, made him terribly appealing. "Tell you what, if this charade actually pays off, you've got your date."

"And if it doesn't?"

"Then you'll just have to think of something else," she said as she turned and stepped to the door, his delighted chuckle putting a smile on her face and extra action in her walk. Once the door closed behind her she sprinted back to her quarters and changed into her uniform before returning to the Security Office.

"Well, you seemed to enjoy your role," grinned Brandon as she came in.

"Shut up, Brandon, you too Suvi-jean; I don't want to hear it. I just hope this worked."

"It will," said Suvi-jean.

Just then the ship's alarm sounded, and the call came. "Security to corridor eight, section three." That was Jake's voice, and they could now see Jonah Thornton on the monitors. He was holding something in his hand and had his back pressed tightly to the wall. Jake was at one end of the corridor and Hal was at the other. Both men were aiming stunners at him.

Suvi-jean, Brandon, and Sheila came pounding up the corridor as the cornered man began to shout. "Get back. Get back, all of you. This virus is deadly. I'll drop it, I swear I will. SUVI 5 get your ass over here and keep them away. Do it or everybody on this ship dies. I'll do it, I swear I will." He was sweating profusely now and weeping as he threatened to drop the glass container.

Hal looked at Jake who nodded. Hal suddenly screamed a challenge and charged at Jonah Thornton. In that instant, Thornton froze, and Jake fired. Thornton's body twitched then started to crumple to the floor, the glass container falling from nerveless fingers. Hal hurled himself at the floor, turning onto his back as he plunged.

The glass fell, and Hal slid along the floor, reaching out. The glass containing the virus dropped into Hal's open hand and he rolled easily to his feet with it held securely. "Easy with that, Hal," said Suvi-jean as Jake hauled Jonah Thornton back to his feet and applied the restraints. "Dr. Reilly's on his way with a secure container for that thing."

"Commander Sorenson, didn't you say the virus wasn't airborne, but transmitted through body fluids?"

"I did, Hal, yes, but that was on the planet. Viruses can, and often do, mutate. Who knows, that might have changed itself, or Farouk may have experimented on it, making it airborne. I wasn't willing to take that chance."

Just then the Doctor arrived, and Hal gently lowered the glass down into the transport container. "Minus twenty centigrade should do it," he mused as he set the dial on the container which began to hum softly.

"We should transport that out into space."

"Jeannie, it'll be perfectly safe in the lab's containment field."

"You're sure about that."

"Yes, I'm fully confident in the safety of the lab. I'd like to study this, but only under controlled conditions. It'll be perfectly safe."

"All right, Doctor, but remember, of the thousands of people on this ship, only eighteen of us are immune to it."

"I'll keep that uppermost in my mind, Ca...Commander." He seized up the container and hurried away.

"What should I do with this piece of misery," asked Jake as he shoved Jonah Thornton against the wall.

"Transport him down to the caverns," replied Suvi-jean.

"Wait, there are laws, rules, I have a right to a trial, you can't ..."

"Take him to transport and put him in the caverns, then contact the Explorer and bring her home."

"Yes, ma'am," grinned Jake. "With extreme pleasure, ma'am. Come on you, get moving."

"Sadly, Suvi-jean, he's right," said Brandon, "he is entitled to a trail."

"And he'll get one, but he can await that day on the planet, not on our ship. We still have to find out exactly who else was in on the conspiracy."

"I get it," said Sheila. "By sending him down you also send a message to those left behind. They'll bend over backwards to blame each other and avoid being marooned on that planet."

"That's the idea," sighed Suvi-jean. "Come on, let's go stand down the general alarm, and then relax in Brandon's office. I have to confess, this has been a strain on me."

Chapter #19

Settling Down

The Explorer settled into her berth and the hatch opened to cheers from the launch bay floor. The crew descended to the deck of the Reacher, to the welcome of Suvi-jean and the White brothers. "Welcome home, family," sang Suvi-jean as she caught a laughing Amanda in her arms. She swung her around and around to make her laugh and shriek.

"Put me down," laughed Amanda. "Jeannie, put me down, we're in uniform for pity's sake."

"Yes, Commander Sorenson, decorum," admonished SUVI 3 as she walked by.

"SUVI 5, about putting Sub-Commander Drake in charge of the Explorer," said Thirteen.

"Yes?"

"It was a good choice. She's an able leader, and she's starting to use her brain. I think there's hope."

"Shut up, Thirteen," said Amanda as she shook a threatening finger at him. He grinned and walked away.

"You two make peace?"

"He's still trying to teach me, but he was supportive as well. I'm starting to like the guy. So, what all exciting happened while I was gone? I assume you found it."

"I did," said Suvi-jean, "or, in truth, Jake and Hal did. They hatched a plan, let Jonah Thornton escape, then when he retrieved the virus, they took him down. I have to admit, Mandy, there's more to those guys than anyone would have guessed."

"Yeah? Tell me all about it."

"Sure, if you tell me what's going on there?" She was looking at the maintenance men carrying a huge crate from the hold of the Explorer.

"What? Oh, that's Lilly's samples. She had me landing everywhere so she could gather samples. In the mountains, on the plains, at the ocean's edge ..."

"The Ocean's edge?"

"Yes, the far south has a huge ocean of poisoned water, teaming with life. Lilly was fascinated with it and all the shrubs, bushes, and whatnot that grew nearby. She had no idea at all of possible danger. Thirteen had half the guys armed as guards and the other half carrying samples for her. She'll be months cataloguing it, organizing it, etc."

"You enjoyed her, didn't you?"

"What? Jeannie, no, I ..."

"Hush now, sweet Mandy, I'm not jealous, I'm pleased that you enjoyed your Command, and your crew."

"Yes, I enjoyed her, her childlike enthusiasm, her excitement, and ... did you just say my command and crew?"

"I did," sighed Suvi-jean.

"Save that for when we get home," said Amanda. "Right now, let's go to the mess for some food."

They arrived to see Jake, Hal, Carla, and Lilly gathered at a table. "Late as usual," grinned Jake as they joined their friends. "Lilly was just telling us about her adventures, telling, and telling, and ..."

"Shut up, Jake," grinned Lilly. "I had more excitement than I could have dreamed of, I gathered a bunch of samples, and it'll take me weeks to sort them all out. I'm happy, I'm excited, live with it."

"I'm glad to see you enjoy your work so much, Lilly."

Lilly and the rest stopped and turned their full attention to Suvi-jean. "Thank you, Commander, I think. What's going on?"

Suvi-jean sighed. "People, just between us, I have to confess, I don't think we'll ever be able to find a planet to call home until we can make one. Each planet develops its own forms of life, as Old Earth did. We outgrew that, but no other planet seems to want us. We're not adaptable enough.

"So, we're going to have to make one. What I mean is, we need to find something close, a breathable atmosphere, survivable climate, etc., but for long term success, we going to have to terraform that planet, make it our own.

"It'll probably take generations to fully accomplish, but it'll be up to Lilly to get us started."

"Me?"

"You. You're the botanist, the Reacher has tons of seeds and samples from Earth in storage. You'll need to explore the possibilities there, as well as whatever you find on the chosen planet, perhaps even incorporate some of what you find on other planets. You'll also want to find us a zoologist that you can work with."

"Commander Sorenson, you're scaring me."

"Oh come on, tell me the idea doesn't excite you, Lilly."

"Excite me? It scares the bejebbers out of me. Well, okay, maybe excite me a little, but ..."

"Lilly, I don't expect you to get it all done by tomorrow. I'll give you a couple of weeks at least."

"Sure, go ahead, laugh at me. First you scare me to death then you laugh at me."

Suvi-jean grinned. "Lilly, yes, I'm teasing you a bit, and I do understand the magnitude of the task I've given you. As I said before, this could take generations, and first we have to find a suitable planet. However, it's up to you to lay the groundwork. What do you think, are you up for it?"

"Well, sure, yeah, but why me? Why not one of the more senior people, someone with more experience?"

"They have more experience, Lilly, but this job requires enthusiasm, excitement for the job, and that you have in plenty. The experience you'll gain as you go, and you can enlist the help of anyone you need."

"Okay, I'm in. Jeez, when I asked for a job I had no idea ..."

"I'll tell you a secret about our Commander Sorenson," said Hal. "Suvi-jean has a certain magic all her own, and you have to be careful what you tell her. Don't tell her your hopes and dreams if you can't deal with having them, because she'll make it happen.

"Look at poor old Jake there, he had a soft job in Sanitation, but he started whining to Suvi-jean, and the next thing you know he's the go-to guy for Security, and Chief of Security for the Explorer.

"And there's Mandy, poor lonesome Mandy, nobody to love, all alone in the transportation room, then bang, Suvi-jean appears riding on a dinosaur and there's Mandy, Chief of Social Engagement, and Second in command aboard the Explorer, not to mention companion to the aforementioned Suvi-jean."

"Wow," grinned Lilly, "so I see. So, what did you wish for, Carla?" Carla didn't respond, she just blushed.

Jake saw and was instantly on the alert. "Little sister, did you have an ulterior motive for stationing me in the Medical Bay when I got my transfer?" Suvi-jean didn't respond, she just grinned and looked all around, feigning innocence. "Why you scheming little matchmaker you."

Suvi-jean laughed and returned her gaze to his. "I don't hear you complaining."

"No, Jeannie," said as he reached for Carla's hand, "I have no complaints at all. I can never thank you enough for all you've done for me."

"So, what did you wish for, Commander?" asked Lilly.

Suvi-jean gave her a gentle smile. "A safe place, a home, friends, a chance to be free, to discover who and what I am. I too have no complaints. This ship, my home, is safe, I have the love of my Amanda, loyal friends, and more. My life is blessed. I ..."

"Senior staff to the bridge. All senior staff to the bridge."

"And there we go," grinned Suvi-jean. "Later, family. Come, Lady Amanda, adventure, excitement, and more await." Laughing, Amanda took her hand and together they headed for the bridge briefing room.

They entered the room to find everyone wearing black armbands. Olga Volkov passed them each one and they put it on. "Grandfather?"

"Jeannie, our Second Officer, Naleen Raveer, has succumbed to the wounds she took during the invasion from the planet. You must now appoint a new Second Officer. This post is a bridge post, Jeannie. You need someone who's an able leader as well as a commissioned officer, someone familiar with the bridge and its protocols."

They were all looking to her now and Suvi-jean remembered the previous meeting where she learned how to command. "First Officer Volkov, your recommendation?"

"Emmet Jones is next in line. I have every confidence in his ability to bring honor to the post."

"Call him in."

"Sub-Commander Jones to the briefing room."

"On my way," came the response which was soon followed by a soft knock on the door.

"Enter," called Captain Baris. The door opened, and a tall thin man limped in and stood to attention. "Sit down, Sub-Commander." He sat.

"As you may be aware," said Suvi-jean, "Second Officer Raveer has passed from this world, leaving her position empty. You've been recommended for the post. Do you accept?"

He looked from Suvi-jean to Captain Baris then back to Suvi-jean. "I do, Captain Sorenson."

"Excuse me?"

"Forgive me, Captain, but for the past few weeks you've been barking orders all over the ship, and even the senior staff have jumped to obey. I'd say the secret isn't much of a secret anymore."

"Well crap," sighed Suvi-jean, "that's a few years sooner than I'd have liked. Are we likely to have a mutiny on our hands?"

"I doubt it, Captain. You led our forces against the rebels, now you've found the saboteurs, and eliminated the threat to the ship and crew. You've forgiven the grounders and brought them aboard. I think you're safe to come out of hiding."

"I don't want to come out of hiding," sulked Suvi-jean. "If I do then Amanda gets to captain the Explorer and have all the fun while I'm stuck here on the bridge."

"The price of command," grinned her grandfather.

"Perhaps not, Captain Sorenson," said the new Second Officer, "your first Officer was once a capable captain in her own right. I know, I served under her for ten years. I think you'd be safe enough to leave the ship in her hands from time to time."

"You think?" asked Suvi-jean, brightening up.

"Convinced of it."

"All right then, I now confirm you in the post of Second Officer and increase your rank to Commander. Congratulations."

"Thank you, ma'am. I'll do my best to bring honor to the post."

"I have no doubt at all that you'll succeed. First Officer, I assume you'll handle the arrangements for Commander Raveer?"

"Already in the works, Captain."

"Then I guess all that's left is for me to announce my retirement," said Captain Baris.

"Not just yet, Grandfather. You served with Commander Raveer, I'd like you to officiate at the ceremony, then give it a few days." He nodded his agreement.

"All right, Grandfather, what's on your mind?"

"It's come to my attention that Jonah Thornton's been returned to the caverns, is that right?"

"You know it is, Grandfather. I had no choice, he's mad as a hatter and dangerous to boot, not to mention a possible rallying point for dissenters. Is this what it's going to be like? I have to be captain, but you'll be watching over my shoulder at every turn?"

"Yes," he grinned.

"Thank you for that," she said as she gripped his hand and returned his smile.

"Commander Hoffman, how's our cleanup operation going?"

"Pretty good, actually. We've seized several weapons, a few substances of questionable origin which were sent to the lab, and a bottle of rare whiskey which I personally confiscated. We've also sent three more people down to the caverns to await their trial."

"So, you plan to give them a fair trial?"

"Yes, I do, Grandfather. No SUVI, including me, can fairly sit in judgement, you're retiring, so that task will fall to the First Officer."

"Saw that coming," sighed Olga Volkov. "All right, Jeannie, I'll do it."

"Then I guess that just leaves one piece of business. Amanda Drake, I now promote you to the rank of Commander. Since you will be primarily in command of the Explorer, you need to carry full command rank. Do you accept the post?"

"I do, Captain."

"So, is there anything further? No? All right then, carry on, people. I'm off for several hours of sleep."

* * * * *

"What's the matter, sweetheart?" asked Amanda as the cuddled into bed.

"It all fell in on me, Mandy," replied Suvi-jean, her voice betraying the fear and uncertainty she'd shown when first aboard the ship.

"What fell on you, honey? What do you mean?"

"Everything. We were just starting to be sweethearts then Grandfather brought up the grounders and it all went to hell from there. Everybody looks to me to make things right, and it scares me, plus we haven't had five minutes alone to explore the sweetheart thing. I'm scared I'll get like my mother and ignore you, that you'll be hurt, or mad at me, or find somebody else to cuddle with, or ..."

"Hush now, sweetheart, hush now, Mandy's got you." Amanda cuddled the distraught woman in her arms and crooned soothing sounds. "I'm not feeling neglected, I'm not mad at you, and I don't ever want anybody else to cuddle with but you. Hush now, sweet Suvi-jean. Let me kiss you, make it all better."

She held Suvi-jean gently and kissed her, holding the kiss until she felt the woman in her arms respond. When their lips finally parted she began nibbling on Suvi-jean's earlobe. "Mandy, what are you doing?"

"Distracting you, dear. Taking you mind far away from those nasty things that trouble you. Is it working?"

"Yes," came a soft reply.

"Good, then I'll keep doing it," chuckled Amanda as she began to kiss and nibble her way down Suvi-jean's throat.

"Amanda?"

"Yes, my sweet?"

"What're you doing now?"

"Practicing my distraction techniques."

"Oh, okay," replied Suvi-jean as Amanda's breath caused her to shiver with a strange delight. Amanda nibbled open her lover's night gown and began slowly kissing her way down her body.

Suvi-jean groaned and squirmed under those sweet kisses. "Amanda, are you trying to make me have sex with you?"

"Absolutely. Is it working?"

"Please don't."

"Sweet Jeannie, I swear I will never hurt you, not ever. Tell you what, if I do anything you don't like, or if it hurts in any way, just tell me to stop and I will, I promise."

"All right, Mandy, I'll do this for you. I'll be really still and do what you tell me."

That was the voice of a frightened little girl and it broke Amanda's heart to hear it. She popped up in the bed and cuddled the girl in her arms. "Oh my poor sweet love, I don't want to hurt you, and I don't want to scare you. I just want to do things that you like. How about we start again with a kiss. If you like that I'll do something else and you can tell me if you like it or not, okay?"

"Okay, I'll ..." Amanda sealed her lips with a kiss, but this time she allowed herself to put more passion into it. Suvi-jean groaned and responded to the fire of that kiss. "Well, did you like that?"

"Yes, I liked that."

"Okay, now this ..."

A while later Suvi-jean lay spent in her lover's arms. "Mandy, my god, what was that you did to me?"

"That, my sweet darling girl, was sex the right way. Did you like that?"

"It did strange things to me, it made me feel funny inside, and now I'm all sleepy. I think I actually exploded and got put back together."

"Then I did it right," chuckled Amanda.

"Mandy, I can feel you're still tense. How can I help you?"

"It's all right, sweetie, just go to sleep and let me hold you."

"No, I think I'm supposed to make sex for you now. Can I do that? Make you all sleepy like me?"

"Tomorrow, sweetie. Your turn to do it to me tomorrow. Just go to sleep now and let me hold you."

"Okay," she said, snuggling into Amanda's arms. "You'll have to teach me how to do it for you."

"It will be my great pleasure to do so, sweet Jeannie. Honey, we shouldn't ..."

"I know. Sex is something we do where nobody can see us, and we never talk about it where they can hear us. That's going to be harder to do now that I know how much fun it is."

"Hush now and go to sleep," chuckled Amanda.

Chapter # 20

Captain Sorenson

The next day was quiet, the day after was the day of the memorial service for Second Officer Raveer and the rest who had perished during the failed invasion of the ship. The ashes of the slain were spread out through an air lock by a crewman in a space suit, then a memorial beacon was set in place, a tiny metal moon endlessly orbiting an inhospitable planet.

Two days after that the trial of Jonah Thornton and four of his co-conspirators concluded. Thornton and three of the others were sentenced to exile on Elysium, the fourth was allowed to return to the Reacher on compassionate grounds, he had a wife and three children. He agreed to the terms of return and was accepted.

The goods and other property of the four exiles were returned to them as well as weapons and some medical supplies.

The next day Captain Baris called the Senior Staff to the Bridge. They stood outside where he could easily be seen on the ship's monitors. Suddenly his image appeared on giant screens throughout the ship, and his voice carried through the ship as well.

"Attention, all ship's personnel, attention all ship's personnel. This is Captain Baris speaking to you for the final time as your Captain. The day has come for me to retire and step aside for younger and more energetic leadership to take over. After twenty-eight years at the helm, I now step down.

"By common consent of the Senior Staff, your new captain will be Captain Suvi-jean Sorenson. Captain Sorenson, the ship is yours."

Stunned, most of the people on the ship watched as Captain Baris shook Suvi-jean's hand, stepped back, and saluted her, then turned and left the bridge. Suvi-jean, wearing a new captain's uniform, turned to face the camera.

"Attention all ship's personnel, this is Captain Sorenson speaking. I did try to convince Captain Baris to remain at the helm for a few more years, but he would not, so you're stuck with me.

"I will now tell you what I hope to accomplish as your captain. Recently we discovered another failed colony on Elysium, however, it wasn't a human colony, it was alien. Those people, whoever they were, abandoned this planet long before we arrived, but they left us a gift, a star chart and map.

"They couldn't tell us where they were going, but they did tell us where they'd been. Since they obviously could breathe an atmosphere similar to what we breathe, we've decided to backtrack their progress, see if any of those planets will meet our needs.

"Our goal is now, as it's always been, find a home where we can survive and thrive. We're the last of the human race, we must endure, survive, and grow strong again. To accomplish this aim we must all work together for the greater good.

"When I finish speaking, the ship will reorient itself to the new trajectory and we will begin preparations for departure. I wish you all well, and a safe journey, as we search for a home among the stars. Sorenson out."

The big screens went blank, and the ship was suddenly abuzz with speculation. Suvi-jean sighed and allowed her shoulders to sag. "I'm glad that's over with."

"You did fine, Captain," smiled Amanda as she brushed lint from the captain's sleeve. "You were awesome."

"Sure I was. Commander Hoffman, are we clear of troubles from the former colonists?"

"I believe so, but I still have a few under surveillance. Should I call that off?"

"Up to you, I trust your judgement."

"Then I'll keep an eye on them for the time being."

Suvi-jean chuckled. "Dr. Reilly, are you doubly sure that damn virus is secure."

"I am, Captain. Nothing to worry about there."

"I hope you're right. Helm, is our new heading laid in?"

"Aye, Captain Sorenson, heading laid in."

"Bring her about and align her along that heading. Commander Jones, you have the bridge. Come, Amanda, let's head for the mess and something to eat."

"Ah, Captain, I'm afraid the captain's mess is that way."

"The captain's mess? Oh no, we're not doing that just yet."

"Captain, we have to," said Amanda. "There are certain things that a captain has to do ..."

"Then you take the job."

"Nope, sorry."

"Fine then," she grumbled as she reached for her comm. "Captain to Ensign Jake White."

"Here, Captain."

"Gather some food and meet me aboard the Explorer."

"On my way, Captain."

They walked along in silence for a while, getting stared at by everyone they passed. Finally, Amanda spoke. "Jeannie, honey, what's going on?"

"Mandy, I will not isolate myself from the rest of the crew like that. If I can't lead, hold their respect and loyalty, by being myself, then I'll pass the job on to someone else."

"Okay, but you'll have to do something about the captain's chef."

"Oh, for pity's sake. Look, all that can wait. Our favorite table at the main mess can be designated the captain's table, and we can still share food and companionship with our friends there. I have an ancestor who was a successful captain, a Viking raider. He ate, drank, and caroused with his warriors, pulled at the oars with them, and fought beside them.

"I love my grandfather, I do, but in this case, it's the old Viking who I'll use as a guide, I like his style better."

"All right, sweetheart, we'll start there. Your style will evolve as we go, and that's as it should be."

They arrived at the Explorer to find Jake and Carla waiting with a large container of food. "What's up, Jeannie, the Captain's Mess a bit quiet for you?"

"Jake, you have no idea. Actually, Mandy and I have been talking about that. I plan to be a bit more accessible than Grandfather was, more visible."

"Yeah, he wasn't always like that," said Amanda. "I remember as a child he was often seen about the ship, but as time went by, and planet after planet failed to be useful, he withdrew more and more into the inner sanctum."

"People started blaming him for the Universe's lack of compassion?"

"Something like that, I guess. Sweetie, a lot of people were putting all their hopes on this planet. It was a good idea to share the star chart with them, give them something to hope for and believe in after having their hopes dashed on the rocks of Elysium."

"Yes, that's something else I plan to do, keep the entire crew somewhat informed as we go along. Farouk Bladon loved his secrets, so did Second Prime. That always kept people at each other, we need them to work together."

"Good luck with that," sighed Jake.

"Thanks, big brother, I'll probably need it. Okay, looks like the inspection of the Explorer is done. Lock her down then get ready."

"We leaving now?"

"Yes. I want to get away from that accursed planet as soon as I can."

"Yeah, you did from the start," smiled Amanda, "and if we had, we'd have saved ourselves a lot of grief."

"What's that you told me," grinned Suvi-jean, "leave the past where it is and step forward? My lady Amanda the beautiful, would you care to step into the future with me?"

Amanda laughed and took Suvi-jean's arm. "I'd be delighted, Captain Sorenson."

Chapter #21

Into the Future

As they neared the bridge, they encountered Captain Baris and a group of maintenance men carrying containers. "Grandfather, what's going on?"

"I'm moving out."

"Moving out? We're on a spaceship, where could you go?"

"I've chosen quarters near Engineering. Moira is going to help me rebuild my old hover speeder."

"You're not serious? Grandfather, you'll break your neck on that thing, I've seen it."

"Well I'm not going to ride it on the ship."

"Grandfather, why are you moving your quarters?"

"Jeannie, you're the captain now, those are the captain's quarters. The cleaners are there now, they'll be all ready for you and Amanda to move into by tomorrow." The look of distress on her face melted his heart and he put his arms around her. "Jeannie, it's all right. This is the way it has to be, and I'm fine with it, hell, I'm happy about it.

"I feel years younger, just getting the responsibility off my shoulders. You're a far better leader than I ever was, and I'm thrilled to pass the torch to you. I'll always be here for you, and you have Amanda to help guide you. You'll be fine, and so will I." He hugged her then released her.

Suvi-jean sighed and gazed into his smiling face for a moment. "All right, Grandfather, as long as you're okay."

"I'm fine, Jeannie, I am. Come along lads, this way."

With a smile and a wave, he was off down the corridor. Suvi-jean stepped onto the bridge with mixed emotions. She felt the hand on her arm give her a gentle squeeze and she shook off the mood. "First Officer, is the ship ready?"

"Ship is prepped and ready, Captain."

"Close all shields. Second Officer, is the bridge ready."

"Bridge is prepped and ready, ship prepared to sail, Captain."

"Helm, engage the star drive."

"Aye, Captain, star drive engaged, charging, charging, and the star drive is ready, Captain, course laid in."

"Hit it."

The helmsman moved a small lever and the ship thrummed for a moment, then set out. One moment it was hanging there above a deserted planet, a silvery satellite orbiting a rock in the dark and empty void, and the next it vanished as it suddenly hurtled through time and space at greater than the speed of light.

On the bridge a young captain stood silently, her thoughts racing, as she tried to absorb the magnitude of the task she'd set for herself.

The End

Echo of the Past

(Book two of Forgotten Worlds)
by

Prudence MacLeod

Chapter #1

Final Entry

Struggling to draw breath, Morthel forced down the well of sorrow and fear. Gently patting the cold dead form of her lover, she fought to draw breath and continue her diary entry. "Antha has gone now, she has not drawn a breath for some time, and she grows cold. I'm the last survivor.

"It's only been a day since something hit the planet, stripping away much of the atmosphere, and pushing us out in the system to a deeper orbit. The power has failed, and the cold of space is creeping in.

"The collision destroyed two thirds of the fleet, so only a chosen few could leave the planet. Even though thousands were killed by the quakes some people still had to remain behind. I lost the draw of lots, and sweet Antha wouldn't go without me. She stayed with me and so we will lie here, side by side for all eternity.

"I hope someone will find this diary one day and know by it all the joys of the colony, and of its sudden and unexpected demise." She pulled her dead lover closer as the racking cough from breathing the frozen atmosphere took her life, the diary still gripped tightly in a hand that no longer trembled from the cold.

Time passed, and the broken colony lay quiet on the surface of a planet that could no longer sustain life. Ages rolled by while the small shelters gazed toward the sparkling stars, the feeble light of the now distant sun no longer able to warm the planet. Eventually, even the beacons failed and stopped sending out their pleas for help, dust settled, and bodies disappeared beneath it.

Eons passed before the silent shelters felt another footstep, but these were larger feet of a different species, and even if the machines had power, the strange new voices would not have been able to activate them.

* * * * *

The small ship, Explorer settled to the frozen ground and spilled out her crew. They began to search through the ruins, eventually arriving at the resting place of Morthel and Antha.

"Carefully, now, Mr. Sacumbtu, carefully. We want to keep anything we find fully intact."

"Understood, Commander Drake. I've about got the doorway cleared now. I'll use a vac blower to suck out the dust and blow it away, so we can see what's inside."

Great clouds of dust rose into the cold thin air and drifted away as he worked. The same for three others who worked at different shelter domes nearby. Eventually he turned off the machine and called out to his leader. "Commander Drake, I think we're ready here. Do you want to go in first?"

"You know I do," she replied, excitement clear in her voice.

Light penetrated the small habitat for the first time in eons, casting eerie shadows as the tall explorer entered and cast the beam around the first room. As she entered a smaller room she found Morthel with Antha held in her arms, still embracing, frozen in that pose of eternal love and death.

"Holy smokes! People, I've got mummies here. Do we have any way to protect and transport them back to the Reacher?"

"Lilly here, Commander. We can use one of my sample crates. There's nothing alive here for me to take home."

"Thanks, Lilly. Bring a crate and a couple of guys to carry it. We'll have to be ultra-careful; I have no idea how brittle these guys might be. We'll have to keep them cold too."

Another woman soon arrived with two men carrying a large crate. The two mummified bodies were gently loaded inside, she set the environmental controls, then the men took the crate and stored it aboard Explorer One. While this was being done the commander checked in with the rest of the crew.

"Report, people, how are we doing?"

"Thirteen here, Commander. We've found lots of tech, probably junk, but we're salvaging it anyway."

"Three here, Commander Drake. I've got something on sensors about a kilometer away. It almost looks like a ship. Should we check that out?"

"Indeed we should. Take Hal and Thirteen with you, Three."

"On our way."

Commander Amanda Drake watched as her ship rose into the air and slowly moved away. When it stopped, she could still see it, but only just. She still marveled that the SUVI, super powered former slaves all, still retained their slave numbers as names by their own choice. The air supply of her enviro suit was running low before her ship returned. She ordered everyone back inside then sealed it up tight.

With a sigh of relief Amanda removed her helmet. "Ah, fresh air at last. Three, take us up to a stable orbit then everybody relax; we'll grab a meal then see where we are from there."

They gathered in the seating area of the small ship and enjoyed a meal of warm rations. "I wonder what's really in this stuff," mused one of the maintenance men.

"You don't want to know," chuckled another.

Amanda smiled as she listened. They'd endured two weeks crammed inside the small ship only to arrive at a cold frozen planet. A planet that had suffered a catastrophic event far in the past, by the size of that crater on the far side of the world.

This side had held a few surprises though, intact habitats, lots of alien tech, and several damaged ships. The settling dust from the main event had covered and protected the ships nicely. She sighed as she finished her meal and began the conversation. "Hal, Thirteen, report. What's the story on the alien ship?"

Hal White, security man on this mission shook his head and replied. "For the most part, it appears to be mainly intact, but it obviously took a major hit and wouldn't fly, otherwise they'd have used it to escape the planet."

"Thirteen, your thoughts?"

The SUVI held no rank by their own choice, but Thirteen was Amanda's self-appointed bodyguard as well as her teacher. "I think it'll be a bugger to get off the ground."

"What??? No, don't say it. Hal, if he tells me to use my brain, shoot him." Both men chuckled at that. "All right, we came looking for alien tech, there's a shipload of it right there, we can't explore it or its potential while wearing enviro suits, so the answer is to take it with us and explore it in the Reacher's cargo bay. Ensign Whang, you're the chief engineer, how do we get that ship home to the Reacher?"

"The short answer is, we tow it. The hard part will be to get it into space."

"Will our transporter shift it out?"

"No, it's half buried under rock. We'd burn out the transporter trying to shift that much mass, but if we can get it loose we can grapple it to the Explorer and take it home that way."

Amanda thought for a moment. "What about the rock holding it down, can we move that with the transporter?"

"No, same problem."

Amanda sighed and looked thoughtful, then she saw the grin on Hal's face. "Okay, Hal, what did I miss?"

"We have a couple of laser drills with us, maybe the boys would like to play."

"How about it, Mr. Sacumbtu, you guys think you can cut away the rock?"

"I haven't seen it," he replied, "but I can't imagine why we couldn't."

"All right, we have a plan. Lilly, have you tucked in our passengers?"

Lilly Peters, the ship's botanist, sighed. "The lovers are in cold storage, Commander."

"You look disappointed, Lilly."

"I'm a botanist, and this is a dead planet, nothing for me to do. My crates are full of mummies and alien tech instead of unique and interesting plants. I'll admit it, I'm a little bummed out."

"Relax girl, once we get back to the Reacher we'll be on our way to a whole new planet, and I'm told it's right where it's supposed to be. You'll have lots to do, don't worry."

There was a round of chuckles at that, then SUVI 3, ship's pilot, put the ship in a standard orbit and everyone retired to the sleeping quarters.

Pale sunlight had barely reached the damaged ship when the explorers returned. An hour later the laser drills had removed the offending rock, the grapple lines were attached, and for the first time in millennia, the wounded ship rose from the ground. It was half a million years too late, but Morthel and Antha finally escaped the planet of doom.

Don't miss out!

Visit the website below and you can sign up to receive emails whenever Prudence MacLeod publishes a new book. There's no charge and no obligation.

https://books2read.com/r/B-A-ZKBBB-DZYPC

BOOKS 2 READ

Connecting independent readers to independent writers.

Also by Prudence MacLeod

Forgotten Worlds
Suvi
Echo of the Past
Survivors

Watch for more at https://www.prudencemacleod.com/.

About the Author

Jennifer Crandall writes and publishes under three different names, Prudence MacLeod, J.L.Crandall, and Jenni Leigh. Learn more about her on her website,

Read more at https://www.prudencemacleod.com/.

www.ingramcontent.com/pod-product-compliance
Lightning Source LLC
Chambersburg PA
CBHW020944180626
46814CB00003B/918